W9-DEV-615

NEMESIS

A TALE OF THE EMERGENCY AND OTHER STORIES

RAMARAO ANNAVARAPU

notionpress
.com

INDIA • SINGAPORE • MALAYSIA

Notion Press

Old No. 38, New No. 6
McNichols Road, Chetpet
Chennai - 600 031

First Published by Notion Press 2019
Copyright © Ramarao Annavarapu 2019
All Rights Reserved.

ISBN 978-1-64546-795-3

This book has been published with all efforts taken to make the material error-free after the consent of the author. However, the author and the publisher do not assume and hereby disclaim any liability to any party for any loss, damage, or disruption caused by errors or omissions, whether such errors or omissions result from negligence, accident, or any other cause.

No part of this book may be used, reproduced in any manner whatsoever without written permission from the author, except in the case of brief quotations embodied in critical articles and reviews.

Disclaimer

All characters in these stories are fictional. Any resemblance to persons living or dead is purely coincidental.

Contents

Preamble

The seventh and eighth decades of the twentieth century were special for our generation in many ways, and for those of us who happened to live in the Eastern and North Eastern parts of the country, life became a traumatic, unforgettable experience. The period covered three wars with neighbouring countries, origin of a new revolutionary concept, emergence of a political creed relying on vote banking, corruption and hired goons, conversion of bureaucracy into a meek and submissive instrument of political will, birth of a new nation on our Eastern borders and a spell of dictatorial governance, sans the freedoms guaranteed in the constitution.

It was a time of chaos and confusion, of fear and apprehension. Normal flow of life and the modern conveniences that made it possible were rudely interrupted by the spread of an unforeseen creed that called for a cessation of ongoing functions in society and an overthrow of the system of governance. A small spark ignited by a group of leftists in a remote village in North Bengal, inspired by the life and writings of a Cuban revolutionary, had spread like wildfire across the state and beyond. When the first reports arrived of agricultural labourers assaulting and ejecting their landlords, called *kulaks* in the report, it was dismissed as an aberration, a freak incident deserving no more attention than a common theft. But the spark kindled in Naxalbari was no will o' the wisp. It spread far and wide with a rapidity which surprised even its innovators. In Calcutta, a group of students forced a medical practitioner to cut down his consultation fees. The success of this operation emboldened the youngsters and very soon their activities and methods began to be felt by others who, in the eyes of the activists were fleecing the public with their greed. At first the movement lacked direction. It was more like pranks played by idle youth, borrowing ideas from newspaper accounts of similar movements elsewhere.

Teenaged students were starry eyed at the simplicity of the Naxalite philosophy. Cheap food, housing, schooling and medical facilities could be assured by simply eliminating all intermediaries who profited in the process, including politicians, corrupt government servants, and greedy merchants, exemplified by the *Marwadis*. If the police came in the way they could be eliminated too. They were no match for the committed Naxalites, proved by the fact that the latter had successfully snatched fire arms from police on many occasions.

With increase in adherents to the new ideology, violence gripped the state. Calcutta's spicy night life came to a stop as the city downed its shutters at dusk. Chowringhee Road and Park Street remained deserted. Bands of armed youngsters roamed the streets and occupied public buildings. Sounds of gun shots and dying screams were heard over the gloomy darkness. Bodies were found in street corners and in ponds. Stations were torched and station staff threatened and forced to part with station cash. The general public reacted with fear on the one hand and tacit support on the other for some of the popular measures espoused by the Naxalites, like reducing doctors' fees and prices of essential commodities. Young, armed Naxalites would leave tiffin carriers in the houses of officers and supervisors in railway colonies and demand food for their comrades. Families complied fearing repercussions.

Workers evolved a new weapon for agitations, the *Gherao*, in which they would surround an office or confine an officer to his room indefinitely, even preventing him from using the toilet. On the notice board at important stations, a list of officials who were to be liquidated would be posted. The names of those who had been eliminated would be crossed out in red each day, spreading fear down the spines of the remaining people on the list. Officers, whom the Naxals considered inimical to their ideology were threatened and sometimes murdered in broad daylight. The Railway Officers' Club became unusable, as armed Naxals made it their *adda*. Some railway officers deserted their posts and left for safer havens, never to return. In Eastern Railway's headquarters, discovery of a carbine spread panic. Officers and staff were ordered to leave office promptly at closing time. Armed guards escorted staff buses, their windows shielded by expanded metal grills.

The central government posted regiments of the Central Reserve Police to assist the state police, but it met with limited success. In the public mind, CRP became a symbol of interference by the central government and was greeted with the slogan, *"CRP kutha Bangla chhodo"* (CRP dogs, leave Bengal alone). The violence was controlled only after the army stepped in. The green lawns of the Calcutta Maidan became spotted with the khaki of the army's tents and the streets reverberated to the sounds of flag marches as army seized the initiative and restored law and order.

Railway operations were severely affected, not only by the breakdown of law and order, but also by the mushrooming of a rash of unrecognized trade unions. Employees, distrusting the two recognised trade unions, grouped themselves into associations claiming to represent different categories of staff, each with an agenda inimical to the others. The railway administration refused to deal with them and they in turn resorted to sudden wild-cat strikes to press their demands.

Unsettled law and order and industrial relations led to a severe shortage of wagons for loading coal, vital for the industrial health of the country. High grade steam coal from the Bengal-Bihar coal fields had to be transported across the nation to meet the needs of defence, railway transportation, power production and the manufacture of all materials from steel and cement to paper and glass. Production and rail despatch of coal were controlled by the government with strict orders of priority. Industrial consumers had to submit their monthly requirements through the Director of Industries and wagons were allotted from day to day based on accepted programmes by the Railway allotment office.

Allotment of wagons became an exercise in keeping a balance between different sectors, trying to distribute the distress evenly. Shortages invariably lead to corruption and this period was no exception. After allotting wagons to meet the needs of the priority sector, defence, railways and thermal power stations, there were very few wagons left to allot to industries.

There were reports of closure of some industries and Directors of Industries in the states began to inflate their needs in the hope of getting a greater share of the allotments. Coal agents, representatives of industries and state governments thronged the corridors of ER headquarters soliciting wagon allotments, using every possible means to influence decisions. The coal allotment office was flooded with recommendations from original sponsors as well as their bureaucratic and political bosses. Obviously, profit margins and commissions for middlemen were sky high. Attempts to help the needy in a fair and sympathetic spirit were distrusted by others and led to complaints of corruption.

On the heels of the Naxal movement, came the army crackdown in East Pakistan, the genocide killing close to a million people. Hordes of refugees entered West Bengal with harrowing tales of oppression. While the army was preparing for all eventualities the monsoon, and melting Himalayan snows, caused severe floods in Bihar and West Bengal impeding the movement of troops, arms and ammunition. When war broke out, Eastern Railway bore the brunt of traffic, handling refugees, troop movement to and from the front and finally the evacuation of Pakistani POWs from Bangladesh at the end of the war.

In June 1975, the central government declared a state of emergency throughout the country. Important leaders of the opposition and their affiliated trade unions were imprisoned, leaving the supportive railway trade union of the ruling party as the sole representative of the workers. The government assumed sweeping powers of arrest and detention in the name of maintaining law and order. Not only miscreants, trouble makers and other ant-social elements, but also intellectuals, professionals and even ordinary citizens, who did not agree with the ruling party found themselves behind bars for unspecified periods. The fear of imprisonment pervaded the nation like some detestable plague and all indiscipline vanished like magic. Almost overnight, the Indian Railways found train operations much smoother than ever before. Interference with trains by way of demonstrations, strikes and *bandhs*, unauthorised use of the alarm chain, train robberies and wagon breaking, and even petty thefts disappeared from the scene leaving the railway managers unfettered in their day to day functions. Ministerial staff, long accustomed to trooping into the office nonchalantly any time up to midday and abandoning their duties well before closing time, got into their seats before opening time and stayed in office up to closing time and beyond. Performance indices rose to dizzy heights inducing the government to set up large hoardings exhorting the people, "If the trains can be on time, why can't you?"

Of course, the people could not know, thanks to a muffled press and a government controlled electronic media, that many railway failures, even accidents to passenger trains including casualties were obscured from their view. Overzealous railway managers, out to please the politicians in power for the crumbs of postings and promotions, also played their part in manufacturing, in their fertile brains, at least some of the results claimed. A single party government, with enhanced powers over the population spawned a culture of arrogance in the rulers, and a fawning, spineless and servile obedience amongst the top bureaucrats including railway managers. The victims were the general public and the unprotected railway employees, denied access to any but the official, unquestioning trade union of the party.

<hr />

All but one of the stories in this collection recall these eventful decades. The last story is of the earlier decade. Nonetheless, it is linked with the way the nation progressed following independence. I owe the story ideas for *Cholera* and *The Letter* to my brother Col (Dr) AL Sharma, SM Retired.

Nemesis – A Tale of the Emergency

With the departure of the evening mail, Kamalganj Station Master Kalipada Mukherjee's work for the day was done and he was preparing to close for the day, when the swing doors of his office opened, and a man dressed in white khadi dress and cap entered the room.

"Pai lagee, bade babu" he said sitting down in the chair opposite Mukherjee without waiting for an invitation.

"Jeete raho, netaji" responded Mukherjee, in the traditional way. He was quite used to such unheralded visits from the Secretary of the local branch of the Railwaymens' Congress, the trade union wing of the ruling party. Kamta Prasad, popularly known as Netaji, was a parcel clerk at Kamalganj, of which Mukherjee was the Station Master. While Kamta Prasad addressed Mukherjee with the traditional respect due to him as

one senior to him both in age and in service, Mukherjee recognised the former's importance as a union leader and treated him with deference.

Kalipada Mukerjee was a typical product of the railway age in India. When the first railway line was laid along the Hooghly near his native village, Kalipada's grandfather was the only person with a working knowledge of English. British officers of the railway company picked him up quickly for a job in the company. His father, trained in rudiments of the Morse code at The George Telegraph Institute in Calcutta, immediately after his matriculation, joined his father's railway company as a signaller, retiring as senior inspector in the traffic department. He had all the qualities needed to become an officer on the railway but the colonial policy of the company, preferring Anglo-Indians and Indian Christians to the natives, had left him in the cold. Kalipada was a graduate and had entered the railway as a traffic apprentice, which gave him much greater opportunities to reach the gazetted rank. A year before the imposition of emergency, he became Station Master of Kamalganj station in the Harishpur Division of the Eastern Railway. By his dedication and competence, he had increased the railway's revenues, improved the railway's image in the eyes of its users and ensured peaceful labour relations at the station. During the last railway week Kamalganj won the shield for best kept station on the entire railway and Kalipada was awarded an efficiency badge. When emergency was declared, he followed all legitimate orders of his bosses without question. But it wasn't easy, because there were some people who were interested in using the existing conditions for their own benefit.

Kamta Prasad's origins were totally different. His grandfather was an accountant in the service of an unscrupulous zamindar in Bihar, where his principal preoccupation was to enrich the estate at the expense of hapless peasants, taking advantage of their ignorance and perpetual indebtedness. He had the foresight, and cunning, to steal a pinch here and a pinch there which enabled him to leave his son Biswanath Prasad several fertile acres and two palatial buildings, and a large amount of cash, in addition to his modest ancestral dwelling. Biswanath Prasad was an employee in the state's revenue department, where he attempted to quench his insatiable avarice by fair means and foul, until he was caught red handed and prosecuted. Awaiting the result of the action against him, Biswanath Prasad preferred a vial of poison to the ignominy of imprisonment. Kamta Prasad inherited his grandfather's cunning and his father's avarice and to them added his own hunger for power. All these qualities found their fulfilment through the ruling party's trade union, which Kamta Prasad served avidly. With the declaration of the emergency he found further reason to congratulate himself on his choice of trade union, revelling in the unfettered use of his powers. The icing on the cake came with the appointment of a fellow Bihari to head the division.

◆———◆———◆

Mahip Singh's rather generous hips invited the nickname 'Hips' from his co-trainees in the Jamalpur workshop, which he joined as a special class apprentice at the tender age of sixteen. His father, a loyal civil servant of the British Raj, despairing of his only son ever acquiring the qualifications necessary to serve the British in a suitably important civil or military capacity, sought the help of his white boss to get him a placement. The latter put in a word with his railway chum in the Dinapore Railway Club, over a bottle of Scotch paid for by the supplicant and the boy found himself at Jamalpur. With his Billy Bunter frame and fleshy buttocks, 'Hips' was a natural target of jokes, but he took them all gamely and soon became a popular member of the Gymmy boys club, as they were known. But the acquisition of knowledge was beyond his ken and he repeatedly failed to answer the tough questions in mathematics and drawing, essential for earning a diploma of AMI(Mech)E, which alone could qualify him to attain the coveted position of a Class I officer in Indian Railways. Fortunately, he was in good company, because some of his batch-mates who were in the same boat belonged to influential families. Before long the government waived the condition and the apprentices took up their positions as Mechanical Engineers alongside the successful apprentices and directly recruited engineering graduates.

Mahip Singh adopted a bluff-and-bully style of management which served him well. Departmental bosses ganged up to give him high ratings in their annual assessments so that the department could have an edge in promotions to ex-cadre posts like those of Divisional Superintendents and General Managers. And so, in time, Hips rose to be a Divisional Superintendent. In Kamta Prasad, Hips found an ideal foil, sharing as they did the passion to get rich quick. Kamta provided him the avenues to exploit, ensuring simultaneously, that his own position as the decision-making confidante of the DS was well broadcast particularly amongst his detractors which included the station master of Kamalganj.

◆———◆———◆

"What can I do for you Kamta babu?" Mukherjee asked evenly, controlling his irritation at the unwanted intrusion in the closing hours.

"I need your help *bade babu*" replied Kamta, handing over a sheet of paper to Mukherjee. "These men have to be enrolled as Traffic substitutes.'

There was no mistaking the tone of authority in his voice. Mukherjee scanned the sheet. It contained ten names, two of which he recognised. They had been recommended by the local MLA a few months back, but Mukherjee had declined to oblige him.

A panel of Traffic substitutes was maintained at every station to be utilised during unexpected, short term vacancies of essential railway workers in the lowest rungs. The railway administration had only recently reiterated its instructions on forming such panels. No new name could be included in such lists without the prior and specific approval of the Divisional Superintendent. Mukherjee was sure Kamta was aware of these instructions.

"'Netaji, you know these names have to be approved by the DS first?" said Mukherjee.

"Yes, I know that *bade babu*" replied Kamta blandly, "you leave it to me", and smiled meaningfully.

Mukherjee shuddered inwardly, pursed his lips and held out the list to Kamta.

"I am sorry I cannot oblige you."

Kamta looked at him condescendingly.

"Think it over carefully, *bade babu*. It is for your own benefit. I will see you tomorrow" he said, and left quickly, leaving the list on Mukherjee's table.

Mukherjee remained staring at the swing doors through which Kamta had disappeared, sighed, and resumed the work the visit had interrupted. He spent a sleepless night pondering the meaning of Kamta's parting words. What 'benefits' had Kamta hinted at? Some benefits of working as SM were taken for granted, like the *mamools* for supply of wagons to consignors and the booking of parcels, and the cuts from the handling contractors. Mukherjee had never looked beyond these, but he knew there were others who collected money from the staff, for small favours like occasional leave, convenient shifts etc. Mukherjee hated to exploit the weakness of his fellow workers for money and heartily disliked all those who indulged in the crime.

It was obvious that Kamta expected to make a packet out of the substitutes. He was also willing to share a part, a tiny one to be sure, with Mukherjee. He shuddered at the thought. Not only was the idea of enriching oneself at the cost of the poor applicants repugnant to him but if the matter got reported to the vigilance department he would be in serious trouble. Kamta could be counted upon to deny all responsibility, because the orders would be signed by the SM. Moreover, Kamta had enough godfathers to save him if it became necessary, whereas Mukherjee would be left friendless. People were being jailed under Maintenance of Internal Security Act (MISA) for much smaller offences. On the other hand, if he did not fall in with Kamta's scheme he was in danger of being hounded. Kamta would surely use his influence to get him into trouble. The least he could expect was a transfer to a less important station. It could be much worse. He could be entangled in some false case and harassed. What choice did he have?

He lay awake into the late hours and finally came to a decision. He would not compromise with his principles. If it meant suffering, so be it. The emergency could not last for ever. Already there were strong undercurrents developing to overthrow it. When it was over, surely his voice would be heard. There was also another factor. Mahesh Kumar, the new Senior Divisional Operating Superintendent seemed to be an upright man. He would understand his point of view and protect him from the likes of Kamta. He had met him in their monthly meetings and had come away impressed. His senior colleagues in Harishpur who were closer to the Sr DOS held him in high esteem for his operating acumen as well as qualities of head and heart. He remembered the words of Biren Bhattacharjee, one of the Traffic Inspectors at Harishpur.

"In all my service I have not come across an officer who is so considerate towards his staff despite being fully involved in improving efficiency. In fact, he firmly believes that the secret of success is through gaining the confidence and loyalty of his staff. What is more, he is not afraid of standing up to his superiors if the welfare of his staff is threatened."

Mukherjee felt he could depend on Mahesh Sahib to bail him out if required. He woke up early despite his being late to bed, completed his ablutions and performed his daily *Pooja*. Today the *Pooja* assumed a different meaning. It was more focused, more fervent, more intense as he prayed *Maa Kaali* to give him strength to face the imminent trials, knowing he was on the path of righteousness. When he rose from his *Pooja* seat, he felt imbued with a new strength, a steely determination to face the future in any form.

When Kamta Prasad appeared the next day, Mukherjee told him firmly that he could not oblige him. Kamta stared at him in disbelief. No one had dared to refuse him so far. The glint of metal in Mukherjee's eyes indicated that he could not be persuaded.

"You had your chance Mukherjeeda. Don't blame me for whatever comes to you now" and with that he left.

———◆———

Mahesh Kumar's belated lunch was interrupted by the arrival of Ashruff, the liveried peon of the DS, resplendent in his spotless white uniform, green *kamarbandh* with its shining brass buckle embossed with the IR emblem.

"Bada Sahib salaam diya, saab" he announced.

"Is he alone?" asked Mahesh.

"No *saab*, Kamta Babu is with him."

Mahesh was piqued at the information. Kamta seemed to be with the DS most of the time. And he felt sure the summons had something to with his presence. Of late, Kamta had been throwing his weight about in the affairs of the Kamalganj section a bit too much. He decided to keep the DS and his visitor waiting.

"Please tell him I will come as soon I finish eating" he replied. When the peon had gone, he ate the rest of his lunch and walked slowly to the DS's chamber.

"Come, come, Kumar, we have been waiting for you" Mahip Singh greeted him rather impatiently, from his seat behind the Burma teak table, exchanging a look with Kamta Prasad who was sitting to the left of his table. Mahesh ignored the show of authority. He decided to play it cool.

"Ashruff must have told you that I had just commenced my lunch when you sent for me, Sir" he replied. "Any way what is the urgent matter on which you desired my presence?"

"Kamtababu wants to tell you something about the affairs of Kamalganj" Mahip started.

"If Kamtababu wants to talk to me I am sure he can call on me directly instead of wasting your valuable time, Sir. Is it not so, Kamtababu?" said Mahesh, looking him in the eye. Kamta Prasad winced and could do no better than nod at the suggestion. And the way Mahesh put it, Mahip Singh was left without an argument.

"Well, all right. When can he see you?"

"I am free now Kamtababu. Please follow me."

Mahesh rose from his chair before either of the others could say anything. Kamta Prasad followed him meekly glancing back at Mahip Singh for support, but the latter could only offer a wry gesture of helplessness.

Once they were in his room, Mahesh Kumar offered Kamta a chair and ordered coffee before opening the conversation.

"Well, Kamtababu, what is it this time?" he asked.

Kamta launched on a series of complaints against the SM of Kamalganj, which according to Kamta, were affecting the earnings of the station.

"He has turned down all my suggestions for enhancing revenue and cutting down expenditure, Sir. Moreover, he is openly saying I am nobody to advise him" Kamta concluded.

Mahesh knew what Kamta meant by 'advice'. They were all ideas for corrupt officials to make hay while the sun was shining and were meant especially for the benefit of Kamta and the DS. Mahesh had given specific orders not to accept any advice from Kamta on matters concerning the running of his department. This had irked Kamta because it curtailed his status as 'the unofficial DS of the Kamalganj section'

"I know of your advice, Kamtababu. I am sure you know that the SM is acting on my instructions."

"But, Sir, I had given my advice, in the interests of the administration, and only after taking permission from DS Sahib, and I had told Mukherjee babu about it. In effect it amounts to flouting the orders of the DS."

They were interrupted by the arrival of the canteen bearer serving coffee. It gave Mahesh the time to control his seething anger. Anger against the deviousness and arrogance of Kamta, anger against the complicity of Mahip Singh in Kamta's machinations, anger against the system which permitted such unscrupulous actions. He regained his composure before he took a sip of the insipid concoction which masqueraded as coffee in the office.

"I would like you to understand" said Mahesh when the bearer had left, "No orders pertaining to my department can be issued without my consent, and even if the DS issues any orders directly, they will await my approval before implementation. DS is aware of this and has agreed with this arrangement. So, it is in your own interest to approach me first with your suggestions instead of trying to force the issue through DS."

Kamta stopped sipping his coffee as he tried to understand the firm resolve behind Mahesh's words. He knew that the DS depended totally on Mahesh for producing operating results and for this reason could not afford to do anything against his wishes. Mahesh's strength was his operating expertise which had earned him high praise from the General Manager and even the Railway Board.

"But Sir, how can I face the members of my union if I cannot get my ideas implemented?"

"Kamtababu, I understand that as a union leader you will have to do *pairavi* occasionally, and as an officer I will have to entertain you. But I can only accept suggestions which will benefit everybody in my department and will help to improve efficiency. You will have to let me be the judge of that as I am ultimately responsible for how my department performs. However, I can assure you that it is not my intention to undermine your position in the union."

Kamta had nothing more to say after this clarification but realised that he could not use the DS to force Mahesh to initiate action against Mukherjee. He would have to find some other way. He said his namaskar to Mahesh and left.

It did not take long for Kamta to strike. And the attack was two pronged. Kamta was confident that with the DS eating out of his hand, all he had to do to take care of Mukherjee was to get a written complaint in Mahip's waiting hands. Mahesh Kumar was, however, a different cup of tea altogether. His Class I status rendered him beyond the reach of the administration at the zonal level, up to which Kamta's influence extended. Moreover, Mahesh had built for himself a reputation for honesty and efficiency, which was not easy to dispel. But if a complaint was made against Mahesh to the Vigilance Department, it would start a process which could, at the least, result in considerable harassment to the officer, even if he was exonerated at the end. Also, Mahip could be trusted to use this as an excuse to get Mahesh transferred out of the division and thus remove an obstacle in Kamta's scheme of things.

Mahesh was busy attending to a minor hold up of trains when the long, insistent ring of the DS's intercom claimed his attention.

"Yes Sir" he responded, holding the phone with his free hand, while he cradled the other telephone on his shoulder.

"Kumar, your friend the SM of Kamalganj has to be placed under suspension" came Mahip's rasping voice through the earpiece.

Mahesh didn't like the implied insinuation.

"What did he do, Sir?" he asked.

"Come and see for yourself."

The complaint on Mahip's desk was unsigned. It claimed to be from 'a patriot' and contained several allegations against Mukherjee, among them violation of extant orders by employing persons of his choice as substitutes, without the approval of DS.

Mahesh reread the letter carefully before returning it to Mahip, who immediately retorted,

"Why are you returning it to me? You have to issue the orders of suspension."

"You haven't marked it to me and signed it, Sir" replied Mahesh.

He seriously doubted whether such drastic action was called for on an anonymous complaint, but remembered that during these abnormal days, people were being imprisoned based on whispers, and decided to keep his own counsel.

"Oh! Sorry" Mahip said sheepishly, signed and returned the letter to Mahesh.

The suspension orders came as no surprise to Mukherjee. Ever since his confrontation with Kamta, he had been waiting for the axe to fall but until now he had been tense, not knowing what to expect. He heaved a sigh of relief and promptly handed over charge of the station to the senior-most ASM. He now found time to attend to many personal issues which he had been forced to neglect on account of his official duties. One of them was a visit to the shrine of Baidyanath Dham, taking the holy waters of the Ganga from Sultangunge, to perform the *Abhishek* of the *Siva Linga* there. When he returned from his pilgrimage, he found a message awaiting him from Biren Babu. Kumar Sahib wanted to meet him urgently. Mukherjee wondered what more trouble the message portended, but keeping his trust in *Ma Tara*, he proceeded to answer the summons.

Mahesh received him courteously, offered him a seat and told him the reason for calling him. It was his unpleasant duty to serve him with a charge sheet for the alleged violation of orders. But he assured Mukherjee that he considered him innocent and would do everything possible to save him from punishment. Mukherjee, however, should co-operate by replying to the charges without delay and assisting Mahesh in closing the case as early as possible. Mukherjee remembered Birenda's advice to put all his trust in Kumar Sahib. He nodded in mute assent. Once the formality of receiving the charge sheet was over, he rose to leave but was stopped by Mahesh.

"Why have you not volunteered for selection to the post of Traffic Inspector?" he asked.

Mukherjee was taken by surprise. He had seen the circular letter from the Personnel Department calling for volunteers just before he left for his pilgrimage, but thought he was not eligible as he was already under suspension.

"But I am under suspension, Sir" Mukherjee replied.

"That does not disqualify you from selection" said Mahesh and added "Submit your option form to Biren Babu before you go, and I will take care of the rest."

Mukherjee did not know how to thank him. 'God bless you, Sir', was all he could say, as he left.

◆━━━━◆━━━━◆

Durgadas Dasgupta, nicknamed Douglas by his class in Jamalpur, stared at the letter in his dak pad with dismay. As Chief Vigilance Officer of the Railway, he was quite used to receiving letters, containing all kinds of wild allegations against officers and staff of the railway. What distressed him was the fact that this time the target was one whom he knew intimately, and for whom he had the highest regard. He had first met Mahesh Kumar on the badminton court in Dharampur, where Douglas was then posted as the Divisional Mechanical Engineer. Kumar was not only an excellent badminton player but, as he discovered when he reported to Douglas for training, a dedicated and very honest officer. Very soon, Kumar had established himself as an indispensable part of the railway's operating team but, unlike others in his department, had an excellent rapport with officers of other departments. The respect he earned from them was reflected in his unanimous election as the Secretary of the Railway Officers' Association. Douglas could not imagine that he could commit an act of corruption, or that Kumar could have any enemies who would frame him in some false case. Reluctantly, he called his most trusted enquiry officer and asked him to ascertain the facts.

Parimal Chakraborty had an instinctive animosity towards Class I Officers, particularly those in the traffic department. He seriously believed that it was a serious mistake to hand over the reins of the railway administration to these raw university graduates lacking knowledge of the working conditions at the grass root level in the railways. Moreover, he had become a victim of the vicious, discriminatory promotion policies of the government, which had been framed, and were implemented by the same set of officers, for the specific purpose of benefiting their own ilk. As Vigilance Officer (Traffic) of the railway, he had investigated several complaints against subordinate staff, supervisory staff and against promoted officers, but complaints against Class I officers had been few and far between. He paid extra attention to such cases and took pride in the fact that in all the cases he had investigated so far, the officer concerned had not been able to escape unscathed. The case against Mahesh Kumar, Sr. Divisional Operating Superintendent of Harishpur, which the CVO had personally entrusted to him, appeared to be an open and shut case.

———◆———

Mahesh Kumar had just returned to his office after a strenuous morning in the control office when the public telephone on his table rang. Mahesh picked up the receiver and said 'Mahesh Kumar' as he always did.

"*Arre bhai Mahesh, mai Moti bol raha hoon*", came the voice in the earpiece.

Mahesh recognised the voice immediately but strongly disapproved the show of familiarity in the address of the caller.

"*Main kisi Moti ko nahin jaanta* (I don't know any Moti)" he said and put the phone back on its stand. It rang again almost immediately. Mahesh picked it up again. This time the caller's tone was different.

"Mahesh Kumar *saab*. This is Motilal. It seems you are upset."

"Motiji, I have told you before not to call me at this time. You are welcome to meet me during visiting hours, like everyone else, and tell me your problems. I will do my best to help you, but I don't like your intruding into my working time."

"Sorry, Mahesh *Saab*. I will see you later."

Motilal Nevatia was a coal merchant who had, during the last couple of years, ingratiated himself with senior railway officers by claiming to have political connections. He would find out the personal needs of each officer, befriend him and offer to resolve them with his connections. The gullible amongst them, who were many, believed him and accepted the proffered aid and, in return, would go out of the way to felicitate the merchant's activities, often breaking regulations in the process. Mahesh Kumar had kept him at arm's length and scuttled all the man's attempts to become friendly.

Motilal arrived later in the afternoon and placed his request before Mahesh Kumar. He wanted out of turn allotment of wagons for loading stone for one of his clients and Mahesh Kumar refused to oblige. Motilal made an oblique reference to the possible advantages that could accrue to Mahesh if he consented.

"Are you offering me a bribe?" asked Mahesh sharply.

"Oh, no, Kumar *Saab*, that was not my intention. I know your reputation. I was only suggesting that I could help you to get transferred to Southern Railway."

When he joined Indian Railways, Mahesh had been posted to the Eastern Railway in line with the government's policy of posting newly recruited officers away from their home states in the interests of national integration. The policy had been given up in subsequent years and many officers had used political or bureaucratic influence to get themselves transferred to their home states. Mahesh had also made a request for transfer to the Southern Railway but, in the absence of political support, had depended on his departmental bosses to help him. His dedication to work and ability to produce results had endeared him to his Eastern Railway superiors to such an extent that they had declared him indispensable. His application had, therefore, remained undisposed. Much as he would like to get the transfer, he had no intention of seeking the help of characters like Motilal. He felt insulted to hear the proposition from Motilal.

"How dare you come to my office and make such a filthy proposal" he said, controlling his rising temper. "You can go now" he added, pointing to the door.

"But Kumar *Saab*" Motilal stuttered.

"Leave now, before I call my peon to throw you out"

Motilal shuffled out reluctantly. Before long, he was in the office of Mahip Singh along with the ever present Kamta Prasad.

"*Iska kuchh karna padega, Mahip Singh Saab.* This Kumar is becoming a pain in the neck"

"We were just talking about it, Motiji. Kamta says we should frame him in a vigilance case."

"That is right. Give me a few days. I will find a case that will nail him for good."

———◆———

Mahesh Kumar entered the headquarters of Eastern Railway and proceeded to his chamber in the coal allotment office. He was the designated coal allotment officer. The passage between the elevator and the entrance to his office was packed with people hoping to get an allotment order for loading coal in the following days. They were willing to do anything to achieve their objective.

In his chamber, Mahesh Kumar set his jaw in preparation for the onerous task before him. The door opened and Srikanto Ganguly, the Office Superintendent, appeared with a frown on his face. He announced that there was a visitor in the office bearing a letter from the Prime Minister. Mahesh told him to calm down and usher in the important visitor. He turned out to be a coal merchant carrying a sealed letter in an official envelope of the Prime Minister's Office. The letter, typed on PMO letterhead, was signed by a junior functionary in PMO recommending allotment of wagons to a certain consumer. Mahesh dismissed the visitor and told Srikanto babu to ignore the letter as the signatory had no authority, whatsoever, to issue any orders for allotment of wagons.

"If the PM wants to favour someone," Mahesh said to Srikanto babu, "all she has to do is to convey her wishes to the Rail Mantri. She doesn't have to get a letter written by an underling. This letter is a fraud."

Many officials, including those at the highest levels, literally blackened their hands in providing transport for coal. At one Thermal power station in UP, the sponsors inflated the programmes and carted off surplus coal from the coal stacks for sale in the black market. There was a category called brick burning coal, mostly meant for domestic consumption, that was sponsored by state governments but enjoyed a low priority. Railways could only allot a few rakes on percentage basis, to keep the sponsors happy. This coal was usually sold in the market at high black-market prices.

When a change of guard took place in the central cabinet, the new Minister for Railways issued orders to allot coal rakes for brick burning to a northern state, in preference to production of power, ostensibly to reach consumers in the state before it became snowbound in winter. Most of these rakes were diverted and consumed en route and those who engineered this move made themselves rich. It was rumoured that the price for getting allotment of a train-load of coal for domestic consumption was as high as ten lakhs and that shares went right up to the top in the railway bureaucracy.

When Kamta Prasad heard the story from Motilal he thought he had found Mahesh Kumar's weak point. Motilal used his connections in the coal allotment office to get the information they needed. Mahip helped them draft a letter to the Director, Vigilance in the Railway Board, who lost no time in sending it to the Chief Vigilance Officer of Eastern Railway for investigation.

◆——◆——▸

Douglas Dasgupta read the report submitted by Investigating Officer Parimal Chakravorty in utter disbelief, but the facts stated therein seemed indisputable. Parimal had done his groundwork thoroughly. The files he had seized from the Coal Allotment office clearly showed that orders for allotment of three full rakes of low priority brick burning coal were authorised by Mahesh Kumar. Information collected by Parimal showed that these rakes were diverted en route and delivered short of destination. He had also determined through oral statements that the coal was sold to consumers at abnormally high rates. Parimal was not authorised to question Mahesh Kumar so he had submitted the report to his boss for further action. Disciplinary action against Kumar could not be initiated without the consent of the departmental chief. Douglas called up the Chief Operating Superintendent and fixed an appointment.

Madan Gopal Varma read the documents place before him by the CVO carefully, going back and forth to check the accuracy of the allegations contained in them. When he had finished, he removed his glasses and wiped them with his handkerchief before looking up at a waiting Douglas.

"Looks convincing, doesn't it?" he said, flashing his trade mark smile with an immaculate set of teeth. "However, it does not tally with what I know about Mahesh, what I have seen of him ever since I came to this railway zone. There must be something missing."

Varma's mind went back to his first meeting with young Mahesh Kumar a dozen years ago. After joining the Indian Railway Traffic Service, Varma had been assigned to a railway zone that had predominantly meter gauge tracks, with low levels of traffic. The work was complicated by shortage of coal for which the railway depended heavily on the Eastern Railway, where the coal mines were located. It was a common practice to transfer good traffic officers from such zones to broad gauge railways for their career development. Accordingly, Varma was transferred to Eastern Railway as Deputy Chief Operating Superintendent in charge of passenger traffic and safety.

He got a cold reception when he reported to the Chief, a diehard officer from Eastern Railway who believed that upstarts groomed on other zones lacked the ability to comprehend the operations of the Eastern. One of the first files Varma dealt with was the enquiry report on an accident that had occurred less than ten days earlier. Satisfied with the way the report was prepared and presented, Varma passed it on to the Chief, recommending its acceptance. He got a rude shock when the Chief returned the report with a stinging note that seemed to point to his own lapses rather than those in the report. The note began with an insinuation,

"If you had read the report carefully, *as I have done*", the Chief had written, "you would have noticed the following shortcomings."

When Varma went to see him to discuss the case, the Chief suggested that Varma should visit the site of the accident and acquaint himself with the conditions there.

"You can also take the opportunity of seeing a coal loading area", he added patronizingly.

Concealing his chagrin, Varma returned to his room and called up the safety officer who had submitted the report and made an appointment to meet him. The field visit was rewarding and educative, thanks to the sprightly young man who met him on his arrival at Asansol. He was the author of the enquiry report that had triggered Varma's visit. Mahesh Kumar was well informed and articulate, not only about the work in his charge but also about general working of the division. Varma warmed up to him immediately and later, when he found the Chief hounding Mahesh needlessly, helped Mahesh out of his predicament.

Varma looked down at the papers on his table and sighed. There seemed little he could do to help Mahesh this time. Maybe Mahesh, like others around him, had succumbed to temptation after all. Turning to Douglas, he asked,

"What next?"

"We will have to record a statement from Mahesh" replied Douglas, "But my VO is too junior to interview him. You may, please, nominate one of your senior officers to do so."

"All right."

Varma dialed the intercom.

"Sir" came a voice.

"Step in here for a minute, Ronnie."

A few seconds later, the door behind Varma's chair opened and a fair looking officer entered the room. Ronnie Braganza was from an Anglo-Indian family that had served the railways for several years. He was the first in the family to qualify for Class I service.

"Hello Douglas" he said, on seeing the CVO and took a seat beside him, wondering what the issue was.

"Have a look at this Ronnie" said Varma, placing the file before him.

Ronnie looked at the papers and frowned when he saw Mahesh Kumar's name. He knew Mahesh from the time he reported to Ronnie for training and had watched him grow into an outstanding operating officer, unsullied by scandal, a proud flag bearer of the department in the success story of Eastern Railway. As he read the report, however, he recalled that he had cautioned Mahesh to curb his overconfidence to avoid getting into trouble. He had worked with Mahesh in the coal allotment section also but at the crucial period mentioned in the report, he had been posted elsewhere. It seemed that Mahesh had gone overboard this time. He raised his eyes to his boss and said,

"Looks pretty bad, Sir."

"Indeed, it does Ronnie. I want you to send for him and record a statement before we return the papers to Douglas for further action."

"Will do, Sir" replied Ronnie and left the room with the file.

The summons from the Additional Chief Freight was nothing new. Two to three times a week Ronnie would call Mahesh for some clarification or discussion. When he reached the Eastern Railway headquarters and climbed the stately Victorian staircase to the first floor as usual and turned towards the Operating wing, Mahesh noticed Mahip Singh emerging from the General Manager's sanctum sanctorum, with a hangdog expression, clutching some papers as if his life depended on them. He wondered what was bugging his DS.

Ronnie put Mahesh at ease with a couple of jokes as usual and then showed him the report of the VO. Mahesh read the report silently with an amused expression on his face. He didn't appear to be perturbed to read the serious allegations against him. When he finished reading Mahesh asked,

"What do you want from me, Sir?

"Chief has asked me to record your statement, Mahesh" replied Ronnie.

"Can it wait till tomorrow, Sir."

"I suppose it can; but no further I am afraid."

"That's all I need, Sir."

Back in office, he called Beni Prasad, a longtime colleague and friend who, as a fellow Bihari, enjoyed the confidence of Mahip Singh, and shared the information about his sighting the DS in the General Manager's office. Beni also had reliable sources of information.

"What's bugging the boss, Beni?" he asked.

"Why? What happened?" asked Beni Prasad in turn.

"I was in HO today and saw the boss coming out of GM's chamber holding some papers. He looked as if he was about to faint. Did he get fired for something? I don't know of anything wrong in the division to invite the wrath of the GM."

"I have some news. I will tell you when we meet next" said Beni and they let the subject rest.

The 'news' from Beni Prasad was worse than Mahesh had expected. In his previous assignment, as DS of a division serving the constituency of the then Rail Mantri, Mahip Singh had cultivated the RM to such an extent that Mahip could almost make him eat out of his hand. Profitting from this proximity, Mahip had brazenly breached rules and procedures, protocol and decorum to allow RM and his *chamchas* to earn commissions from every type of activity, reserving a tidy share for himself. Along with Motilal Nevatia, he floated a company in his wife's name to grab contracts. He also ignored the leftist unions in the division and insulted their leaders.

The party high command did not take kindly to the RM's activities and eased him out of the cabinet in the next reshuffle, leaving Mahip without a godfather. This was the opportunity his enemies were waiting for. A complaint was lodged against Mahip Singh with the Central Vigilance Commission with a long list of his misdeeds, supported by evidence. Mahip was sent on leave to await further orders. After a couple of months, he succeeded in persuading his departmental bosses to let him return to duty and was posted to Harishpur division.

The enquiries had now been completed and a charge sheet containing a dozen transgressions had been issued, among them illegal leasing of a railway pond for fishing, allotment of land for activities unconnected with railway working, procedural lapses in the award of contracts, interference in selections of staff for promotions, and the breach of conduct rules in floating a company. The charge sheet had been sent to GM Eastern Railway to be served personally to Mahip Singh. The charges were severe and the evidence clinching. It seemed unlikely that Mahip would be spared.

While Mahip was struggling with the blow to his prestige and the bleak future before him, the country witnessed unexpected political changes. The Emergency was withdrawn and in the elections that followed, the ruling party was decimated, and a labour friendly conglomerate of parties emerged as victors.

Kamta Prasad lost his clout and Motilal Nevatia ran for cover, as the law pursued him. Neither had the time or the guts to commiserate with Mahip Singh, much less help him in his hour of need. Kalipada Mukherji was exonerated of the charges against him and promoted as Traffic Inspector.

On the advice of Beni Prasad, Mahip Singh appealed for a review of the case against him and offered to put in his papers if he was spared the ignominy of punishment. His departmental associates eventually persuaded the new Rail Mantri to let him go. Mahip handed over charge to his deputy and took the evening train to his hometown. When a DS is transferred, the whole division wishes him Godspeed. The DS and his wife are profusely garlanded and photographed and the news flashed in the newspapers the next morning. But that evening, apart from the Station Superintendent, who kept his part of the protocol, Mahesh Kumar and Beni Prasad were the only two officers to see the couple off. Mahip Singh bade them a tearful farewell.

"I don't deserve this courtesy from you boys. I don't know how to thank you" he said, choking on his words.

As they left the station Beni Prasad asked a question,

"What happened to that Vigilance against you, Mahesh?"

"It has been dropped" replied Mahesh.

"I was told it was a strong case. How did you manage to get out of it?"

— ◆ —

In the quagmire of corruption that developed from disruption of railway operations in the wake of the breakdown of law and order, a few officers in the Railway Board, including the member in charge of traffic, kept their integrity intact, shining like white lotuses in a mud pool. To protect officers in Traffic Directorate, and on the railway zones from unreasonable demands from Ministers, MPs and their hangers on, Member, Traffic curtly told the Minister's secretariat that verbal orders on special out of turn allotments would not be implemented. He advised his close confidante, the Additional Director Traffic, to devise effective means to shelter officers from any future probes by vigilance organisations. The ADT in turn reiterated these orders to traffic officers on zonal railways.

"Devise your own methods" he told them, "but save your asses."

Mahesh carefully preserved the original papers in each case, consisting of the beneficiary's request, the note put up by the traffic directorate to the RM, the orders signed by the PS to RM on his behalf and the letter issued by the ADT attaching these papers, leaving typed copies in the file. He kept all the papers in a box file that remained in his personal possession even after he had been transferred to another post. In the file in the custody of the Vigilance Department, the copy of the original orders had been removed. When Mahesh showed the papers to Ronnie Braganza, and in turn to their Chief and the CVO, they heaved a collective sigh of relief and closed the case, not forgetting to congratulate Mahesh on his foresight.

Business As Usual

The season was changing. People brought out their woollens from their naphthalene ball preservations of the previous year. The nip in the air in the mornings was palpable. The coming of Christmas was heralded by processions of carol singers filing through the streets leading to the large chapel in the railway colony, the candles in their hands shining like glow worms in the morning mist. In nearby Calcutta, the shopping arcades in Chowringhee came alight with festoons and brightly lit neon lights announcing attractive discount sales, while wishing their patrons a Merry Christmas. Park Street bedecked itself like an excited, eager bride for the coming festivities.

Ahuja and Vasu exhausted themselves in visiting the colourful sights with their families, in this their first Christmas in Calcutta. On Christmas Eve, the prayers in the midnight mass in the nearby church carried to Vasu's bedroom keeping him awake for most of the night. He went to sleep in the small hours of the morning, and woke up late, to see from his window, lines of colourfully clad Christians making their way towards the church. He lazed for a while before getting up, and when he just finished his morning ablutions, the doorbell rang. It was answered by Banarsi, Vasu's servant. A few moments later, he entered Vasu's room to announce that some Sahib had come to meet him. Vasu found a stranger sitting in the drawing room, behind a pile of packages of different sizes stacked on the centre table. He rose at Vasu's approach. The man was dark complexioned and of medium height. He wore dark glasses, a rich gabardine suit and a loud tie. A wide belt prevented his trousers from slipping from his large paunch. A strong scent of the perfume, he seems to have liberally applied, filled the room. The air of prosperity which the man radiated and the packages he brought filled Vasu with suspicion. He had heard that many of the merchants he came across in his official capacity were quite capable of offering bribes for getting undue favours to further their own selfish interests.

"Yes? What can I do for you?" he said somewhat testily.

The other man broke into a wide grin showing a gold tooth.

"I came to wish you a merry Christmas, Sir" he replied.

"And what are all these for?" queried Vasu.

"Season's gifts, Sir. For you, for madam, and for the children." With that he began to open the packets.

"Don't. Don't open them" Vasu almost shouted at him. "First tell me who you are."

'Sir, my name is HS Sanyal,'

It took a few seconds for Vasu to realise that the man in front of him was none other than the Goods clerk who had been recently shifted to a less sensitive position. His temper rose uncontrollably. He resisted the urge to get physically violent and spoke only after he had sufficiently cooled down.

It had all begun a few weeks ago on an otherwise routine day in the office.

"I think you should look in the Standing Orders, Vasu" said Ahuja peering at Srinivas through his thick glasses.

Santosh Ahuja was the Divisional Commercial Superintendent of the Harishpur Division, the most important constituent of the Eastern Railway, itself the largest revenue earning zone of the Indian Railways. Srinivas was his assistant. They were in Ahuja's office, a square room dominated by a large table, behind which Ahuja was sitting in his revolving chair, Vasu facing him, surrounded by the knick-knacks of bureaucratic officialdom. Several telephones, an 'IN' tray with files awaiting Ahuja's attention, the official railway calendar adorning the wall opposite Ahuja, with holidays marked in red, a board on the wall to his left showing the movements of important officers and inspectors, a blackboard on another wall showing Ahuja's engagements written in chalk by the Office Superintendent. On the floor to his right was a square box into which Ahuja had tossed files after disposal. Behind him was the incumbency board showing the names of all the officers who had occupied the post. Ahuja took great pride in pointing out the names of his illustrious predecessors who had risen to high positions in the railway hierarchy.

Vasu picked up a worn out, well fingered reference book from the book shelf beside Ahuja and began to turn the pages.

"Look under 'w' in the index" Ahuja prompted.

"Yes" replied Vasu and began to read out the entries for Ahuja's benefit.

"war...wells...winter clothing...woollens."

He paused.

"Hey, this one is interesting. 'Women travelling alone at night'" he read, looking at Ahuja with a grin.

Ahuja grinned back. They were good friends. Twenty-eight years old Ahuja had been in the service for only five years while Vasu, who was two years younger, was a year junior in service. They believed that a sense of humour, of which they had plenty, was an essential ingredient of success.

"Stop being frivolous" he chided, good humouredly.

The red telephone rang loud and long. It was the Divisional Superintendent.

Ahuja rushed to pick it up.

"Morning, Sir' he spoke into the mouthpiece.

Vasu could not hear the DS, but Ahuja's side went like this.

"No, Sir ...Yes, Sir ...All right, Sir...Right Sir", and he placed the phone back on the receiver.

"Any trouble?" quizzed Vasu.

"Oh, no, no. Lahiri is with him."

"You mean Byomkesh, the Vigilance man?"

"The same. DS has sent him to see me."

Vasu rose to go. "I will be in my room" he said.

"No. Please stay, I would like you to join the discussion."

"As you wish" said Vasu, sitting down.

Byomkesh Lahiri was an officer reputed to be snooty and unpleasant. As Vigilance Officer, he had the license to poke his nose into the affairs of others, and that had made him even more unpopular. His posture of righteousness and self-importance as the anointed custodian of the railway's conscience, as well as his attempt to project himself as the confidant of the General Manager of the Railway, had left him with few friends. Yet no one wanted to get on his wrong side, recognizing that given half a chance he could create endless trouble for those who crossed his path. Although holding the same rank as Ahuja, his going to meet the DS before meeting the DCS was a deliberate act of discourtesy to provoke Ahuja.

As these thoughts passed through the minds of Ahuja and Vasu, the subject of their joint deliberations entered the room. He was dark and short with furtive, darting eyes behind black rimmed glasses. A prominent middle spread, and the streaks of grey in his moustache, around his temples and in the carefully parted hair betrayed his age.

"Good morning, Ahuja. Hello, Srinivas" he greeted them, more breezily than seemed necessary, his wide grin revealing tobacco stained teeth.

"Morning Byomkesh" responded Ahuja without rising from his chair.

"Good morning Mr. Lahiri" said Vasu, standing up.

After the preliminary pleasantries, Lahiri came to the point. The Vigilance organisation had recently conducted checks in the goods sheds of Harishpur and found several irregularities. A report had been sent to the division advising action to be taken against the staff identified by the vigilance team. It was expected that strong measures would be taken against them by the divisional officers to serve as an example to others. The reply received from the division indicated, however, that no action had been taken so far. This was disappointing and was likely to draw adverse reaction from the GM as it would reduce the impact of the Vigilance team's efforts to root out corruption from the railway. On behalf of the GM he had taken up the matter with the DS, who had advised him to apprise Ahuja of the dangers inherent in delaying action on a vigilance report.

Ahuja and Vasu listened to the tirade in silence, Ahuja struggling to control his temper. It was obvious Lahiri was trying to score a point with the GM against Ahuja. Lahiri had reason enough to do so. He had been angling for posting as DCS Harishpur but his ambitions were dashed when the new CCS had decided to prefer the young, energetic and incorruptible Ahuja. Lahiri wanted to show the GM that posting Ahuja was incorrect.

Both Ahuja and Vasu were aware of the vigilance report Lahiri was talking about. The vigilance department was expected to be specific in its reports, citing definite instances involving corruption, identifying individuals indulging in malpractice, and laying traps for them so that when the divisional management received the reports, they could award exemplary punishments without losing time. The report on Harishpur goods sheds did not conform to these norms. It contained only general observations, hearsay evidence and incomplete details, making any meaningful action futile. Lahiri certainly knew the lacunae in the report but wanted to pass the blame for inaction to Ahuja.

Ahuja would have lashed out at Lahiri if he hadn't read the message in Vasu's eyes advising restraint. Instead, he patiently explained the difficulties in following up the report. Ahuja and Vasu assured Lahiri that the matter would be further discussed with the DS and some steps would be initiated under his guidance. Lahiri took leave pleased with himself.

After Lahiri left, Ahuja and Vasu reviewed the case again and decided to recommend to the DS the possible course of action to avoid any adverse impression on the GM. It seemed to them that the only course open was to identify those goods clerks who had spent the longest time in the same job and to shift them to other positions, less likely to give them a chance to make a fast buck by unfair means. When Ahuja briefed the DS about Lahiri's visit, the latter readily fell in with Ahuja's suggestion. Transfer orders were issued the same day, taking effect from the following day.

If the young managers holding charge of the commercial department of the Harishpur division imagined that they had beaten the problem they had another guess coming. Things began to happen even before the ink had dried on the office order stating that for administrative reasons Sarbasri Himangshu Shekhar Sanyal and Anil Kumar Chaki, Assistant Goods Clerks in Harishpur Goods Shed were transferred to the returns section. The Goods Superintendent of Harishpur, Chittaranjan Mukerjee called on Ahuja to enquire why the two AGCs were being moved. Ahuja told him the background and at the same time cautioned him quite firmly not to try to get the orders reversed, keeping in mind Chitta Babu's links with many senior officers in the hierarchy. Ahuja was known to be intractable in most situations. This was a much more sensitive issue, and Ahuja's message through Chitta Babu was duly conveyed to all the right quarters. At the same time, it was well known that Vasu exercised considerable influence through his friendship with Ahuja, and it was generally believed that the orders were his brainchild. It followed that if Vasu was persuaded to soften his stand, he would take the initiative to get Ahuja to change his mind. And the pressure began to build around Vasu.

First it was a call from his friend and predecessor in the post, Sachin Gupta.

"Hello, Vasu, how's life?" he began. After exchange of the usual banter, he came to the point.

"I want you to do something for me, Vasu" he said.

"Tell me, Sachinda, and it will be done" assured Vasu, unaware of what was coming.

Sachin explained the purpose of his call. He wanted Vasu to talk to Ahuja to review the orders of transfer of Himangshu Sanyal.

"He feels it is a blow to his prestige" he added.

"That is precisely the purpose of the orders, Sachinda" countered Vasu. "Moreover, since the orders were issued by Ahuja, why don't you talk to him yourself? After all you are batchmates. Moreover, you two hold the same rank."

"Well, you know how pig-headed he can be. It is quite useless to talk to him."

"What makes you think he will listen to me?"

"Everyone knows your relations with Ahuja. Also, the Goods Shed is under you. So, if you suggest it, I am sure he will agree."

"That is a bit too much to expect, Sachinda. Sorry, I am unable to help you this time."

All of Sachin's persuasive charms could not break Vasu's resolve and he rang off disappointed.

The next was a call from Girish Ghosh, a senior officer in the department. In the past, his attempts to influence Ahuja had met with curt rebuffs. He now tried his hand on Vasu, who being a junior officer was not expected to show the same attitude as his superior. However, Ghosh had not reckoned with Vasu's unflinching loyalty to Ahuja, and duly drew a blank. Several others jumped into the fray. The local union leader, a local politician and even an emissary from the secretary to the GM. The youngsters in charge were a match for all of them. Without losing their cool, and with the full backing of the DS, they stalled all moves to have the two transferred goods clerks reinstated to their former posts.

Vasu came out of his reverie and looked at the man before him,

"Are you a Christian?" he asked.

"No, Sir."

"Do you think I am a Christian?"

"No Sir. I know you are Hindu."

"Christmas is neither your festival nor mine. Then why did you waste your money to buy gifts for us?" asked Vasu, with a look which clearly told Sanyal that his game was up. Before the latter could recover and reply, Vasu continued, raising his voice,

"You were trying to bribe me to get your transfer orders cancelled. How dare you come to my house? Pick up all those unwanted things and leave my house this minute."

Hearing the commotion Vasu's wife rushed from the kitchen. Seeing her, Sanyal turned to her and said, in an imploring tone, raising his folded hands towards her,

"Madam, please take pity on me. Please ask Sa'ab to save me from starvation. Please make him cancel my transfer."

"I don't interfere in Sa'ab's office work', she told him politely, "please do as he says" and returned to the kitchen.

Sanyal appeared defeated. He tried another angle. He said he could not carry the parcels all by himself, so he begged Vasu to let the parcels stay. Vasu immediately ordered Banarsi to fetch a rickshaw and carry the parcels down to load them into it. Sanyal had no alternative but to meekly follow Banarsi, taking leave of Vasu with a Namaskar.

Vasu mentioned the incident to Ahuja the next day and the facts were carried to the DS and other superiors, all of whom greatly commended Vasu for his conduct. They also appreciated his desire not to proceed against the culprit in order to avoid causing embarrassment to his family. In the past, such efforts had yielded no results, because the accused were able to use the liberal interpretations of the courts on adequacy of evidence to wriggle out of the allegations. Meanwhile the local grapevine buzzed with the news that not only was the DCS a strict officer, but his Assistant was also not purchasable. No further attempts were made to interfere with their decisions, which were motivated by a desire to cleanse the administration and increase efficiency.

In course of time both Ahuja and Vasu were claimed by other assignments outside the Eastern Railway. Returning to Harishpur several years later, Vasu went to the room of Robin Mukherjee, the Station Superintendent to make a few phone calls. Suddenly the whiff of a familiar perfume wafted into his nostrils. Only it was much stronger. Someone addressed the Station Superintendent in a rough authoritative tone. The voice also seemed familiar. Vasu turned slightly in his chair to look at the intruder from the corner of his eye. He saw a man dressed in spotless white khadi, with a matching white cap to cover his baldness. His glasses were gold rimmed and he wore a heavy gold chain round his neck. His mouth was full of *paan*, which made him slurp when he spoke. As Vasu searched his mind to identify him, the man saw him and immediately came forward, smiling effusively.

"Namaskar, Srinibash Sahib, Namaskar," he said, "how nice to see you after so many years. How are you? And how is madam?"

Suddenly, things fell in place in Vasu's mind. This was Sanyal, whom he had unceremoniously ejected from his house only a few years ago. But he seemed to be even more prosperous now, and what was more surprising, more powerful.

"Good morning to you Sanyal. It is nice to see you. And even more to see you doing so well. My wife and I are well. How are you and what are you doing these days?"

"With your *ashirbad* I am well, Sir. I am in a hurry to catch a train, Sir. Sorry can't talk much."

He rushed out of the room but not before reminding the SS to remember his instructions. When he left, Vasu turned to the SS.

"My! How the man has changed! What has he been doing, Robin Babu?"

"When you pushed him out of the goods shed, it became a blessing for him. He immediately joined the Railwaymen's Congress and using his old influence in the goods shed soon became a force to reckon with. He is now the General Secretary, gets a cut from every activity on the railway, has close contacts with all political big-wigs including the Minister of Railways, and throws his weight about as you saw him do a little while ago. Nothing can be done on this railway without his consent, no transfers, no promotion orders, and no new policy decisions. Even the GM listens to him because Sanyal has convinced him that he can get the GM promoted to the Railway Board with his influence with the Minister."

Cholera

General Pushpendra Singh, GOC-in-C Eastern Command, read the Governor's letter for the second time. It gave him immense satisfaction to receive the Governor's thanks. It would be useful when his name came up for selection for Chief of Army Staff (COAS), the top post in the army. But the special mention of a fighting formation unit aroused his curiosity. He pressed a button in the intercom console beside his table. The light above the button lit up immediately and a voice issued from the speaker,

"Morning, Sir" It was the General's staff officer, Col. Manickam.

"Morning, Manickam. Do you know anything about the 3rd Maratha Regiment?"

"Sir. The unit was in Assam last year, after which it was brought into West Bengal for IS (Internal Security) duties. At present it is deployed on the East Pakistan border awaiting further orders, Sir." Col. Manickam rattled off.

That's what Pushpendra Singh liked about his staff officer. He was not merely well informed. He could produce the information at a very short notice.

"Any idea what they have been doing there?"

"Sir. I thought you might be interested. I have a field report here from Lt. Gen. Atul Shukla GOC of 3 Corps. They seem to have done rather well during the floods."

"Bring it in, will you?"

"Sir"

The General ended the conversation and restored the button on the console to 'Off'.

———◆———

The officers and men of the 3rd Maratha Regiment. welcomed the respite from the IS duties, which they had never treated with enthusiasm, but always discharged with the usual efficiency and discipline. They were a part of 7 Infantry Division which was itself a part of 3 Corps, deployed in the Western border in the Indo-Pak war of 1965, during which they had won many awards for bravery. Fired with patriotism, the Jawans found it difficult to reconcile their training for defending the country with using weapons against their own countrymen who, it was said, were threatening the peace of the populace. It was a relief when it was over. Resuming their normal drills for maintaining physical fitness and combat readiness, they relaxed and enjoyed the brief interlude before being recalled to more onerous tasks. The information from across the border sent a wave of nervous expectation among the officers and ranks. They knew they would be called up any time to show their valour to defend the country.

Col. Brij Mohan Chopra called his officers for assessing the unit's preparedness for the imminent tasks. Major Sushil Varma and Major Subhas Chakravarty reported that the troops under their command were fighting fit, relaxed and eager. The Adjutant, Capt. Vilas Bhishikar, assured his Commanding Officer that the morale of every single soldier of the 3rd Maratha was very high, and that they were in fact itching for a fight. Col. Chopra turned to Captain L. Narahari AMC, the army doctor attached to the unit.

"And how is the health and medical front, Doc?"

Captain Narahari was in his late twenties, a dark, lanky six-foot, South Indian, whose appearance belied his mental and physical toughness.

"Everything in control, Sir, except for one thing."

"And what is that?" asked the Colonel, somewhat nonplussed.

"Well Sir, from what we have been hearing, it looks as if we will be going to a place where there will be many refugees presumably living in unhygienic conditions. Moreover, the monsoon threatens to be plentiful this year. There may be heavy floods. Just the right conditions for an outbreak of cholera, Sir. We will need a lot of vaccine. I am afraid we are going to run short."

"But I thought you had checked the stock before we came to West Bengal, doc. Has it been used up? Or, has it become ineffective?"

"Neither Sir. But it is just adequate for us. We will need extra supplies for the civilian population."

"The civilians will have their own supplies, won't they?"

"Yes Sir, they will, but we will be on the spot much before the civilians wake up to the dangers of the epidemic. We can save many lives by taking advance action."

Major Varma, who had been listening to the exchange in amused detachment so far, could not hold himself back any longer.

"Hey Doc, forget the civilians. You are in the military now, remember?"

Narahari resented the interruption.

"I am a doctor first Major, bound by the Hippocratic oath" he replied testily.

Col. Chopra intervened to stop further discussion. "It's all right, Major. I think Doc is right."

Capt. Narahari lost no time in getting the supplies of the anti-cholera vaccine, for which he had pleaded with his CO. He decided to take the help of other military establishments in the vicinity, which he hoped would have some vaccine to spare. The obvious choice was the static Military Hospital (MH) at Panagarh under Hq Bengal Area. Thinking that direct approach would be the best under the circumstances, he drove down the hundred-mile road to Panagarh in his jeep, reaching his destination a little before noon.

In the office of the Commanding Officer of MH Panagarh, Subedar Mohan Singh, the Head Clerk, told Narahari that his CO was away on leave. Narahari decided to meet the JCO in charge of Medical Stores of MH Panagarh to ascertain the availability of the vaccine. Subedar Amarnath turned out to be a genial and helpful person. When Narahari told him the purpose of his mission, the JCO volunteered the information that apart from a reserve of 500 doses of the vaccine in stock, fresh supplies of another 15000 doses was expected the next day. He, therefore, did not expect any difficulty in meeting Narahari's needs. However, since the CO was not available Narahari would have to obtain permission from the Station Commander.

Narahari thanked him for the information and weighed his options. It was not normal for an officer of his rank to call upon an officer commanding a station. At the same time, it would be wasteful to make another trip for the same purpose. Moreover, since the Regiment was expected to move at short notice, he may not get another chance to visit Panagarh. As if reading his mind, the JCO suggested to Narahari to take the help of the DQ, short form of Deputy Assistant Adjutant & Quarter Master General, (DA & QMG), who was Staff Officer to the Station Commander. Maj. Charan Singh, the DQ, welcomed the RMO, heard about his mission and told him that the Commander was away in Asansol for a meeting with the Divisional Superintendent of the Eastern Railway, and was expected back only in the afternoon. He promised to brief the Station Commander to make his job easier.

The Station Commander, Panagarh, Brigadier Sourabhjit Pasricha, of AOC, nicknamed Sourpuss by his peers, had, in addition to his name, qualities, which suited the sobriquet. When he returned to Panagarh that afternoon he was in a worse mood than usual. He had sought the meeting with the railway Divisional Superintendent to complain about the condition of railway service at the Panagarh base, but the DS, an acerbic, squirrel faced South Indian, had turned the tables on him. He claimed that, apart from failing to assist the railways in meeting the Naxalite threat in the last two years, the military establishment at Panagarh had been hindering the railway's efforts to restore normalcy, by continuing to be the most indifferent railway user in the division. He buttressed his arguments with a plethora of facts and figures, which Pasricha never even knew existed. He concluded that, as one who held the rank of Captain in the Second World War, he could very well understand the cause for the lack of efficiency at Panagarh, giving Pasricha the queasy feeling that the man thought him unfit to head the base. The journey back from Asansol had only added to Pasricha's resentment. His jeep had to trail behind a caravan of coal trucks all the way up to Chiriya More, and later, when he had curtly ordered his driver to step on the accelerator, the idiot had got stuck behind an oil tanker for the rest of the distance. At home, his wife, who was the headmistress of a local school, had left for work, leaving him to eat a cold lunch all by himself.

It was well past 3 PM when he strode into his office. Maj. Charan Singh recounted the events, which had occurred in his absence, mentioning the visit of the army doctor from the fighting formation at the end of the briefing. To Pasricha, his words were like the touch of a hot iron applied to his high-strung nerves. The mention of fighting formation brought back bitter memories. It reminded him of the ignominious retreat in the war with China, and of his flight for life, unmindful of the safety of his men. After the war was over, he was charged with dereliction of duty and cowardice in the face of danger, and offered the choice of leaving the army in disgrace or accepting service in the Army Ordnance Corps. He had opted for the less risky postings at static stations in the AOC and found his erstwhile colleagues in the infantry supersede him to become Major Generals, while he languished as a Brigadier.

Pasricha's journey into the past was interrupted by Maj. Charan Singh's question,

"Shall I send him in, Sir?"

Pasricha signalled his assent with a slight wave of his left hand.

When Narahari entered he saw a man older, and certainly larger than he expected, but what struck him most was the fact that his face was as red as ham. Through the narrow slits formed by his swollen eyelids and bulging cheeks, his hostile eyes glared at him like a pair of no entry signs. Steeling himself for what might follow, Narahari drew himself to attention and saluted.

"Captain Narahari AMC reporting, Sir" he barked in the best military style.

"Yes?" Pasricha asked petulantly.

"DQ must have told you, Sir" began Narahari.

"Speak for yourself, young man" snapped Pasricha.

Narahari was not expecting a warm welcome, but as a visiting officer, even though of a lower rank, he deserved some courtesy. He realised the meeting was going to be difficult.

"I am Medical Officer of the 3rd Maratha Regiment. Sir, presently on active duty at the Eastern border. We are running short of Anti-Cholera Vaccine. I am here to seek your help, Sir, in replenishing our stocks, as regular supplies may be delayed. I am sorry to trouble you Sir, as the CO MH is away, and the need is urgent."

"We have no surplus. I am sorry" replied Pasricha and started to look at the papers on his desk, indicating that the interview was at an end.

Narahari bridled at the lie and the way he was being treated. Throwing caution to the winds he said, barely masking his resentment,

"Sir, I have checked up from the MH. You have 500 doses in reserve, and your stock is likely to come in a day or two. We are expecting orders to move to the border area any minute, so if you could give me these 500 doses, I will be able to immunise my troops before we move."

Pasricha trembled with rage.

"When I said I don't have any surplus, I mean I don't have any surplus. Is that clear?" he shouted, so loudly that the DQ rushed up from his room to investigate.

Narahari clicked his heels at attention briefly, turned and left the room.

Maj. Charan Singh found Pasricha gesticulating wildly.

"Get that fellow here this minute" he ordered Charan.

"Who, Sir?" asked Charan, bewildered.

"That Amarnath, who else?" shouted Pasricha, as if the whole world knew whom he had in mind.

For the next half-hour, Sub. Amarnath received a chastisement he would never forget in his life. He was accused of being disloyal, of leaking important secrets to an outsider, and of being insubordinate.

Colonel Chopra was wild when he heard about the reception Narahari was given at Panagarh. Immediately, he shot out a signal to the Headquarters of 7 Inf. Div. stating that his troops could not move because there was no cholera vaccine, giving in some detail the role, played by Stn. Hq. Panagarh. Narahari next contacted the medical representative of 7 Infantry Division, located at Kanchrapara, who immediately sent an ambulance with 500 doses of cholera vaccine.

He also visited the civil hospital, where he managed to get another 500 doses. In response to Col. Chopra's signal, another consignment of 500 doses also arrived within a few days. When he had finished inoculating his soldiers, Narahari had enough vaccine and to spare, a luxury that he would soon find becoming a necessity.

Soon afterwards the signal came to move the unit to a place called Ghoshpara, on the road to the town of Jessore, in Eastern Pakistan. Ghoshpara was a small hamlet, beside a meandering rivulet, aptly known as Bankanala, which had a channel disproportionately large for its size. But it was said that in the rainy season, it had enough water to fill the channel and more, which it drained into the Sharada River, a tributary of the Bhagirathi. The 3rd Maratha Regiment set up their camp on the high ground overlooking the Sharada River. Reccy parties surveying the surroundings found communities of the newly arrived refugees living in clusters, on the banks of Bankanala as well as Sharada. It was only a matter of time before they would become victims of the unsanitary conditions in which they lived.

The rains came in early June and poured down in torrents. Mercifully the cyclonic disturbance which had developed in the Bay of Bengal spent itself off before it crossed the coast but the depression which followed settled itself over Bengal and Bihar for a week, drenching the plains relentlessly. Drains turned into raging torrents, and the sleeping Bankanala, aroused like a passionate woman, embraced its banks and overflowed into the Sharada. Together, the two rivers filled the low-lying areas around them, the Bhagirathi adding its own overflow and created a huge expanse of water, submerging the villages. With the water rising under their feet, the villagers scampered to the safety of the high grounds near the military camp, hastily grabbing whatever they could salvage from their submerging homes. The newly arrived refugees were the worst hit, their temporary shelters made up of tarpaulins, polythene sheets, and jute bags washed away in the rains.

Col. Chopra ordered his men to come to their relief immediately, without waiting for a request from the civilian authorities. Relief parties were formed consisting of jawans and a few youthful volunteers from among the villagers. Narahari and the men from his medical unit provided medical assistance. The first task was to attend to the injured and to immunise everyone from the possible outbreak of cholera. Fortunately, Narahari had enough vaccine left after inoculating his troops to suffice for almost all the villagers and the refugees. The relief parties then imposed a modicum of hygiene and sanitation to keep the temporary shelters as safe as possible.

With the abatement of the rains, the level of the waters dropped, giving the civil authorities a false sense of complacency. But worse was to follow. The heavy floods in the Ganga, which had been ravaging the higher reaches of the river during most of the previous month, now reached the east. The Bhagirathi swelled up menacingly, pushing back the waters of the Sharada and the Bankanala, which in turn spilled the excess into every brook, drain, road and lane of the villages on their banks. Within a few hours, the landscape was converted into a vast, muddy, swirling lake filled with jetsam from the villages the water had destroyed. Roofs of houses, trees, bloated carcasses of drowned cattle and even human bodies floated in the water or were washed ashore. The only dry places were the military camp and the railway station, which was on a high bank.

When the waters receded this time, the residues left behind by the rivers caused havoc amongst the survivors of the floods. Shortage of drinking water, infections from the putrefying flesh of the dead, and the general lack of cleanliness brought on the outbreak everyone had dreaded. Thousands fell victim to the epidemic before the government could respond to the call for relief. People died like flies, as the men of the 3rd Maratha Regiment. mounted their relief operation. They ferried people to safer locations, distributed rations, fed them wherever possible and gave them medical aid. Narahari and his band of volunteers worked day night providing succour. The volunteers, and most of the villagers and refugees of Ghoshpara, escaped the epidemic thanks to early immunisation.

When the government reviewed the impact of the floods and the effectiveness of the relief measures, a surprising statistic came to light. The percentage of flood victims and cholera victims was lowest in one remote village at the confluence of Bankanala and the Sharada. The report of the District Magistrate of Nadia detailed the valiant efforts of the small band of volunteers led by the men of the 3rd Maratha Regiment and attributed their success to the foresight of the officers of the army outfit in inoculating the villagers well in advance. The Governor of West Bengal wrote to the GOC-in-C Eastern Command to thank him for the invaluable assistance of the army in meeting the emergency caused by the floods. He remembered to make a special reference to the role of the 3rd Maratha Regiment.

General Pushpendra Singh closed the folder containing the report of Lt. Gen. Shukla and returned it to Col. Manickam.

"Any suggestions?" he asked.

"Sir. I think the boys deserve a pat on the back"

"You are right, specially that youngster, Narahari. Put up a citation. But we must also write to CO Bengal Area to record a displeasure in Brig. Pasricha's file"

"Will do, Sir" replied Gen. Manickam, standing to attention.

Once again, Brig. Pasricha missed his promotion.

The Wooden Staircase

The hot summer sun appeared later than usual, hidden by grey murky clouds. It had rained heavily in the early hours of the morning. Humidity, always high in this part of the year, rose to near saturation. People woke up from fitful slumbers, drenched to the skin in their own sweat. Suburban dwellers, rising early and rushing through their ablutions to reach the nearest rail heads in time, found themselves slowed down on roads inundated by flooded, overflowing drains. Irate passengers, travelling in overcrowded trains, running late due to signals failing for wet track circuits, arrived at their destinations at the edge of their tempers. Scared ticket collectors abdicated their duties. Following a time-honoured practice, passengers lined up at the office of the Assistant Station Master, to obtain 'late slips' for their respective trains to claim attendance in their offices. All in all, it was a normal day in June for Calcutta. Or so it seemed.

But today was different. The first indication was the refusal of the railway staff to issue 'late slips', the crowd being forcibly dispersed by an unusually large contingent of the Railway Protection Force. In the Commercial Offices of Eastern Railway, situated in Dalhousie Square, late comers learnt with surprise that the Attendance Registers, which were usually kept in the chamber of the Assistant Officer in charge, had been sent to the new Deputy Head of the Department, said to be strong disciplinarian, and that they were expected to sign them in his presence.

Mahesh Kumar watched them as they trooped into his room in single file, sheepishly, eyeing the pile of Attendance Registers beside him covetously. He felt sorry for them. Even in normal times, the pressures of urban living forced them to arrive late for their work. Conditions were particularly bad this morning. He noticed their wet clothes, and their mud-splattered *chappals*, *dhoties*, and cloth shoulder bags.

"I am sorry, friends, but you must have heard that the government has declared a state of emergency throughout the country. I am under orders to enforce the existing rules of late attendance."

He went on to remind them of the rules. Once the Attendance Register was removed to his room, a cross would be placed against the names of all those who had not already signed. All those who signed later would lose half a day's leave and if they turned up more than an hour late, they would be marked absent. He placed the Attendance Register before them.

"It is also my duty to caution you that the government has assumed full powers to deal with defaulters with a stern hand. I would, therefore, advise you to follow the instructions to avoid getting yourselves into trouble."

They listened to him sullenly. Except for two union activists who preferred to take the day off, the rest signed the register and trooped out of the room one by one.

During the lunch break, Mahesh Kumar mentioned the incident to his boss, the Chief Claims Officer, a disciplined Tamilian called K. Keshavan, better known as KK. Keshavan chuckled to himself and then observed,

"Nothing works like the cudgel in this country, does it?"

Mahesh knew that a remark of this kind meant that Keshavan's memory cells had been jogged. He waited, while his boss marshalled his thoughts and reminisced.

◆———◆———◆

Reminds me of an incident that occurred about two decades ago, began KK. At that time, I was working in your post. It was then called DCS (Claims). When R. Sridharan was CCS, we developed a very good rapport, so when he was transferred, he advised his successor, who had come to work in Calcutta for the first time, to entrust all his problems, personal as well as official, to me while he settled down.

At the mention of Sridharan, Mahesh recalled the face of a pleasant Malayalee gentleman, ever courteous and considerate, even to new comers in the railways like himself.

The new CCS, continued KK, was S. Somasekharan Iyer (nicknamed SS), a tall well-built South Indian. He was a national level wrestler. He had spent his entire career on the Southern Railway, so he was quite unfamiliar with the work culture in this part of the country. A few days after he joined, he sent for me and asked,

"I say KK, what is all that noise?"

It was around 11 AM. I could hear a thumping noise coming from the direction of the wooden staircase, which served as the main entrance to the office. I used to hear it every day and thought nothing of it, but I realised that for him it was an unfamiliar sound.

"They are the footfalls of the staff climbing up the stairs, Sir" I explained.

"Why are they climbing the stairs now?" asked the boss.

"They are coming into the office, Sir" I said.

"What do you mean they are coming to the office? They should have been here an hour ago."

I tried to play it down without sounding patronising.

"Well, in Calcutta, Sir, they usually get delayed for one reason or another. It has become the practice to permit them to come late."

"How dare they come so late? This must stop at once. From tomorrow, anyone who arrives after the permissible time shall be marked absent. I will personally tackle the late comers."

He was as good as his word. The next day all officers were told to close the attendance registers at ten minutes past ten. SS called me to his room at ten-thirty to confirm that his orders had been carried out. After that he led me to the top of the staircase to await the latecomers. Just as it neared eleven, a group of clerks sauntered noisily up the wooden staircase as they had always done, unaware of what awaited them at the head of the stairs. As the first of them emerged, SS advanced swiftly and hauled him up, holding his collar in a steely grip.

"How dare you come so late? Don't you know the office opens at ten?" he bellowed at the hapless victim.

The man tried to blubber something, but the sheer shock and surprise of the action left him speechless. Those who were on the staircase stopped in their tracks, dumbfounded. They had never seen this hunk of a man, who seemed to have emerged from thin air to grab their colleague, like an ogre in a fairy tale. Finding himself master of the situation, SS released the man he was holding and addressed the latecomers, in a commanding tone,

"All of you have been marked absent. You can return to your residences now. From tomorrow, make sure you arrive on time."

With that, he turned on his heel and marched to his room, with the air of a general who has worsted the enemy in a one-sided battle. I hurried after him. As we entered the room, he turned towards me and said triumphantly,

"See, all it needed was a show of strength."

He strode to his desk, sat down in his revolving chair and beckoned me to a seat opposite him. He pressed the call bell to summon his peon and ordered coffee.

"This calls for a celebration" he said and proceeded to expand on the need to maintain discipline at all times, citing examples of his success in restoring order wherever he had worked before. I sat staring silently at my coffee cup, without applauding his performance. Finding no encouragement from me he queried,

"Why KK? You don't look satisfied."

"Sir, we cannot get physical in this place. I am worried about the fallout" I ventured.

"What bloody fallout? I am not afraid of anyone."

I could visualise him flexing his muscles to meet any situation.

We didn't have to wait long. There was a commotion outside the door, and before SS could press the call bell to summon the peon, the door was thrown open and a group of men trooped in unceremoniously. I recognised among them the leaders of both the unions, walking side by side, which was rare. They crossed the long room and approached the table where we were sitting. SS, who was initially taken aback at this intrusion, regained his composure. Before any of the entrants could open their mouths, he addressed them in the ringing tones of a commander chastising his troops.

"How dare you enter my room without my permission?" he demanded.

It was the turn of the union leaders to be taken aback. They and their followers stopped and involuntarily stepped back. Those in the rear left the room quietly. Seeing their hesitation, I beckoned to the leaders to leave us for the present and meet me later in my chamber. They obeyed reluctantly.

When they left, SS called his office superintendent and told him to frame charge sheets against the union leaders, and their hangers on for indiscipline. I tried to dissuade him, but he would have none of it.

"These bounders must be put in their place" he said.

The stirring events in the Commercial Department were soon heard in the corridors of the General Managers office. The top leaders of both the unions pressed the Chief Personnel Officer to get the orders of CCS rescinded and the charge sheets issued to their union-mates withdrawn. The GM, a canny Punjabi civil engineer, battle scarred in dealing with labour, sent for SS. He congratulated SS for his bold action in the interests of discipline. At the same time, he stressed the benefits of pulling back as a strategy in labour relations. We cannot make the staff, and the unions, our permanent enemies, the GM told SS, particularly in regions where people in general tend to be volatile in displaying their emotions. Finally, SS was told that the CPO had devised a face-saving formula, which would enable the administration to close the issue, without causing embarrassment. SS had to publicly apologise to the staff for taking law into his own hands. SS was unwilling but the GM persuaded him that it was in his own interest to follow the advice of CPO.

SS was a changed man after this incident but decided to seek a transfer back to the Southern Railway. The staff of the Commercial Department heaved a collective sigh of relief and resumed their old habits, unhindered by the whims of inexperienced outsiders.

———◆———

"The Government seems much more serious this time, Sir", said Mahesh, when KK had finished his narration.

"I hope so", said KK, with a tinge of doubt in his voice.

The severity of the orders and the firmness of the management's resolve to enforce them soon became evident to the employees, who for the first time since the country gained independence from foreign rule, began arriving in office well before the scheduled time. But the artificial idyll was not to last. Growing discontent internally, and worldwide condemnation of the rape of democracy in the name of national security, forced the government to withdraw the emergency and restore democracy. As expected, the ruling party was routed at the polls that followed. With the release of trade unionists, social workers and the rest, life returned to its former chaotic state with a vengeance. It took another mid-term poll to erase the aftermath of the emergency. A chastised nation gradually groped its way back to normalcy.

A few years down the line, Mahesh was back in the Commercial Department of Eastern Railway as the Chief Claims Officer. His boss, the newly appointed

Chief Commercial Superintendent, was a product of the Western Railway. He had managed to scuttle all attempts to transfer him out of Bombay for over two decades. He went only when he was sent abroad on a lucrative assignment. When he returned, he was posted to Calcutta, following the railway administration's new policy, which made it mandatory for all officers returning from foreign assignments to serve in the eastern part of the country, for a specified minimum period.

Mahesh entered his office and settled down to work. He hardly reacted to the usual thumping sound from the wooden staircase an hour later. There was a ring on the boss's exclusive intercom.

"Morning Sir", said Mahesh, into the speakerphone mike.

"I say Mahesh, what is all that noise?"

The Letter

It was a time of celebration in the Officers' mess of the 3rd Maratha Regiment. They had just registered the first important victory against the Pakistani Army in their drive towards Jessore. It had been much easier than expected, and earlier than scheduled. The Pakistani army in East Pakistan had been engaged in controlling the rebellion in East Pakistan on the one hand and countering the guerrilla tactics of the Mukti Bahini on the other. Consequently, it had not been able to pay adequate attention to the defence of Mushirhat, a provincial trading centre, on the western border beyond Jessore. The Pakistani Commander of Jessore, learning of massive deployment of Indian troops on the Indian side of the border, had sent patrol parties to secure the borders, as well as to glean more information of the Indian positions. One such party, in its zeal for collecting information had crossed onto the Indian side, near the fortifications manned by the 3rd Maratha Regiment. The alert sentries of the unit had detected the violation of the border and ambushed the patrol party, resulting in the death of a Pakistani officer and a few soldiers. The rest had surrendered.

The body of the slain Pakistani officer was searched, and all documents and personal belongings seized before it was repatriated to the Pakistanis. The papers betrayed the weakness of the Pakistani defence of Mushirhat and hastened the decision of the Indian army command to push towards Jessore. The rest had been easy. With the Mukti Bahini keeping the Pakistanis at bay and the common people cheering the Indians on, the 3rd Maratha Regiment overran the town with practically no resistance.

As each officer entered the Mess, the bearers greeted them with,

"Badhai Ho Sarkar"

"Mubarak Ho Huzoor"

The officers made straight for the bar where the bartenders found their clients more boisterous and demanding than usual. They were also hailing and congratulating each other warmly. In the absence of the Commanding Officer, Colonel Brij Mohan Chopra, who was held up for reporting on the events of the day to his superiors, Major Sushil Varma, received the felicitations, as his colleagues surrounded him recounting incidents and regaling the company with the highlights of the action. The entry of Captain Patel caused a commotion. Everyone, including Major Varma stood up to greet him, because he was the one who led the sortie against the Pakistani intruders, and paved the way for the Indian victory.

After the initial greetings, Major Varma asked him,

"Well, Capt. Patel, what did you find on the Paki, apart from the official documents?"

"Like what Sir?" Patel said in answer.

"I mean his personal belongings" clarified Varma.

"There was some Pak currency, Sir. And yes, a photograph, probably of his wife, and a letter written in Urdu"

"Seems interesting. What did you do with them?"

"I turned everything in, of course"

"This could provide some entertainment. Let us get them here" Varma ordered.

A short while later, a sealed packet marked, 'Personal belongings of Captain Israr Ahmed, Pak Army' was laid on the table before Major Varma. He opened the parcel carefully and extracted from it a slightly frayed but clear colour photograph of an attractive young woman. He examined it and then pronounced,

"Kudi Soni Haigi" (The girl is beautiful)

There was an immediate rush of outstretched hands as everyone wanted to see the picture. Varma passed it to the next man in hierarchical order, and as the photo changed hands, each officer added his comments.

"Wow"

"Kya Baat Hai"

"Hai Main Mar Jawan"

"Haye Mera Dil"

And so on. Captain Narahari AMC, the unit's doctor, viewed the proceedings with increasing anguish and disgust. When the photo was passed to him, he looked at it and silently passed it on to the next outstretched hand. When the photograph was returned to Varma, he had already taken out a letter from the package in front of him.

"Does anybody here know Urdu?" he asked.

"I do, Sir" said a voice in a distinctly Punjabi accent. All eyes turned to a young Sikh in the assembly.

"Lt. Hardit Singh at your service, Sir" he said, stepping up to where Varma was seated.

Varma handed the letter to Hardit Singh. A circle was formed round him and Varma. Everyone waited with bated breath for the entertainment to begin.

"Mere Sartaj" read the young Lieutenant, *"Aaj tabeeyat kuchh nasaaz hai. Jaane kyon dil rah rah ke ghabra raha hai. Sochti hoon ki apko dil ki baat khat mein likhoon to shaayad sukoon aaye."*

Hardit Singh paused for effect.

"Aye haye kya likhti hai" said one.

"Please translate each sentence as you read it" said another.

Most of his listeners could understand Urdu to some extent because of their exposure to Hindi film songs, but there were some that were quite unfamiliar with the language. Hardit obliged them.

"My lord, today I am feeling restless. I don't know why my heart is filled with fear. So, I thought, maybe, if I write to you about my feelings, I will get some peace of mind. My anguished heart burns, and the clouds of smoke that rise from it settle in my eyes to cause torrents of tears. My whole body is afire, thirsting for your gentle caress. Singed by the heat of my longing, my hair dries up and refuses to be dressed. My parched and caking lips are pining for the sweet nectar of your kisses.

"*Id* has come and gone but you haven't come. The cruel moon laughs at me and asks, 'Where is your *Id ka Chand?*' I bought new clothes for the children for *Id*. They refused to wear them without you. With great difficulty I persuaded them that you will be here for the next *Id*."

There was more. She wrote about her daily chores, her troubles with the maid, her trivial problems that she would have told him when they were together. At the end she wrote.

"*Meri Jaan, Mere dil ke maalik, Khuda se roz yehi dua karti hoon ki 'Ya Allah, mere mehboob ki khair ho aur agle Id tak mere dil aur jism ki aag bujhane unke aane ka samaan karna'. Khuda Hafiz. Aapki Mehbooba Fatima*", which Hardit Singh translated as,

"My life, lord of my heart, every day I pray, 'Oh God, protect my beloved and arrange to send for his return by the next Id to quench the heat of my body and my heart.' Your beloved, Fatima."

Hardit read the letter slowly, savouring each word and reading a second time when he or any of the listeners found it juicy. At the end of each sentence, and its translation, he paused for his audience's reaction. There were loud cheers, bawdy jokes and even some lewd comments. It seemed that, starved of female company, as they had been for a long time, they were enjoying the vicarious pleasure provided at the expense of the dead soldier's hapless widow.

Captain Narahari did not participate in the revelry. From the beginning, he had felt that the whole thing was in bad taste. He bore with it with an expression of disdain and, as the reading proceeded, kept his gaze rivetted to the floor. He squirmed in his seat when he heard demands for a second reading, which was accompanied by more boisterous laughter, bolder remarks about the writer's person, and flights of the listeners' imaginations. When there were loud shouts for a third reading, Narahari, who was indignantly waiting for this revolting display of insensitivity to end, could not restrain himself any longer. He stood up and shouted at the top of his voice,

"I say stop it. Haven't we degraded ourselves enough?"

His outburst was greeted with a stunned silence. They all stared at him in open-mouthed disbelief.

As the presiding officer, Major Varma felt impelled to show his authority.

"Hey Doc" he called, "take your seat. This is not a medical problem."

Narahari refused to be cowed down.

"But it is a human problem" he retorted angrily, "a problem of ethics, a problem of decorum. Are we inhuman? Have we no shame? What are we all laughing at? A wife's letter to her husband, a soldier, a martyr, a patriot, who died fighting for his country, even if that country is presently our enemy? Can we deny that each of us fighting for our country could meet the same fate? How will you feel if the letters of your wives, your fiancées, your girl friends are ridiculed in the same way?"

Colonel Chopra had entered the room quietly when the second reading was nearing completion. He had heard the doctor's reaction and Varma's response. He now entered the centre of the surprised circle and spoke,

"Officers, the doctor is right. It is a pity none of you had the sense to think like him. I thank God he is here today to put an end to this nonsense. We must not forget that we owe a duty not only to our country but also to humanity. We must honour the dead, ours as well as those that belong to the enemy. We must respect their families, just as we have a right to expect them to respect ours. Ask your conscience whether your conduct this evening has been worthy of officers of the Indian army."

There was no more conversation. The officers avoided looking at each other and resumed their activities in a subdued, sombre mood. Col. Chopra collected the letter and other belongings of Capt. Israr Ahmed and returned them to his office.

The next day Col. Chopra wrote a letter to the widow using his company's letterhead.

"Dear Madam,

I regret to inform you that your husband Capt. Israr Ahmed was killed in the course of an ambush in our locality. He died a soldier's death on the field of battle. His body has been returned honourably to the Pakistani army authorities, in terms of the Geneva Convention. Please accept my sincere condolences on your bereavement. Should you need any help at this end, please do not hesitate to write to me. I would be only too glad to be of any service to you.

Yours sincerely

Chopra BM, Colonel"

To make sure that the Pakistani censors do not intercept the letter he sent it to the military attaché to the Indian High Commission in Islamabad, with a request to have the letter delivered through non-official channels.

When she received the letter, Fatima Begum did not believe the news of her husband's death. The Pakistan government, underplaying its army's reverses in East Pakistan, had withheld information on the loss of their army personnel from their families. But her last letter to him and her photograph, which were enclosed with the Indian Colonel's communication, left no doubt about the veracity of the statement. When peace was restored the Pakistani army also duly advised her that she had become a widow.

Lost and Found

The oppressive, brooding silence that hung upon the railway yard was broken by the sound of the engine whistle several hundred meters away. Not the shrill joyful notes of a steam engine but the lethargic, dragging hoot of an electric locomotive, like the plaintive protest of a bovine nudged out of its marshy haven. Other sounds followed. From the direction of the engine a distant rumble, like rising thunder, grew in volume and identified itself as the sound of couplings responding to the pull of the locomotive, transmitted down the length of the goods train like a line of recruits responding to the roll call. As the train started moving, flood lights in the railway yard covered the men standing along the track in a play of light and shade, revealing their oil-smeared uniforms and their perspiring, exhausted bodies. The torch lights in their hands threw a beam of light on the under-gear of the wagons, searching for the slightest defect, their ears striving to hear the faintest discordant sound that could make the train's journey unsafe. When the train gathered speed they could see, in its rear, a dismembered green light moving sideways and when it came nearer, they discerned in the flashes of light falling on the brake van, the outline of the guard waving the green light towards the driver. Head Train Examiner, Rangarao led the men back to the washing rooms to change into mufti before heading home. The train passed safely and as the men relaxed, the station clock of Chandichowki chimed eleven-thirty, indicating that they had been working for ninety minutes overtime to get the train ready to meet the midnight deadline.

The loud clang awoke Nagamma dozing on a straw mat near the front door of their three-roomed railway quarter. She lifted her frail, famished body, visibly under some severe mental stress, opened the door and looked out. The dimly lit passage between the row of quarters was as lifeless as it was when she had seen it an hour ago, all the quarters dark, their inmates having retired to bed long ago. Even the animals had stopped scuttling around and found their respective resting places. The scene depressed her further. Inside, her twelve-year old daughter Radha was in deep slumber unaware of the turmoil in her mother's mind.

It was quite normal for Rangarao to be delayed beyond midnight whenever he was in the evening shift and Nagamma used to await his return cheerfully so that they could share their meals. But tonight, her heart was gripped by a nameless fear since the time their sixteen-year old son had failed to return home even at ten PM. Her worst fears seemed to have come true. She had concealed her fears from her daughter and gone about her household chores in a daze.

After Radha went to bed, she spread the mat near the front door and fell on it exhausted by the tension in her being. Evil foreboding about her son crowded into her mind and squeezed her heart so tight that she could hardly breathe. But the clock reminded her that Rangarao would be home soon. She struggled to reach the bathroom to wash her tear stained face and be ready for him. She stared in disbelief at the stranger looking back at her in the mirror. There were dark blotches below her red, swollen eyes. Her skin, once smooth and shiny was now wan and sagging, the wild strands of her silky black hair were in complete disarray. Desperately, she made herself less alarming to her husband's sight and walked back to the front door and opened it. There was still no sign of Rangarao. Her heart doubled in weight. She bolted the door and slowly slid down against it and passed out.

Her delirious brain conjured up all kinds of horrors until she could hear a loud pounding in her head. Slowly she came to and realised it was her husband knocking. She rose to open the door, her resolve to conceal her feelings forgotten, as she saw his figure silhouetted in the moonlight. Rangarao noticed her intense suffering, entered quickly and asked in alarm,

"What is the matter? Why are you looking so pale? Is Radha all right? Where is Jogu?"

"It is nothing" she replied quickly composing herself.

"Then why are you looking so sick?"

"It is only that I am worried about Jogu."

"Well? What about him?"

"He hasn't returned home yet"

"Did he tell you where he was going?"

"He said he was going to Avinash to study as usual, but I don't know...." She trailed off.

Ranga placed a finger under her chin and raised her head. He wiped her tears and said softly,

"Come on Nagu, you worry too much. You know he has changed. It is not the first time he decided to sleep in Avinash's place because they lost count of time in their studies. Let us eat first. I don't know about you, but I am starving."

She held his hand on her cheek for a second feeling reassured, turned and got busy with the chores of serving and eating. The load, lifted from her chest with Ranga's arrival, looked for a new parking place.

Ranga went to freshen up before eating. As he washed, the droplets of water splashing on to his face shone line tiny stars in the bathroom light. It reminded him of something. Yes, he remembered with a flash. The lighted ends of cigarette butts in a dark night. His right palm ached, and the tiny droplets felt like hot embers as the memory of its impact on Jogu's tender cheek surged out of his conscience like a tidal wave.

———◆———

Ranga was in the evening shift that day. He was not expected home till near midnight. When he opened his locker, he realised that he had left an important document at home and decided to retrieve it when there was a lull in the workload. He was able to do so only after dark. As he crossed the railway yard, lighting his way with a flashlight, he noticed a small cluster of lights behind the railway quarters to his right. Glowworms, he told himself, but something in their movement caught his attention. He remembered that it was not the season for glowworms. Suddenly, a small light glowed and moved sideways, revealing the face of someone lighting a cigarette. Ranga froze as recognition dawned. It was his own fifteen-year old son Jogarao. Switching off the flashlight to avoid detection, he moved towards the group cautiously. He was greeted by a raucous laughter of one of the boys which he recognised as that of Vicky, the spoilt brat of the yard sweeping contractor and the accompanying sniggers of his hangers on. Vicky had grown into a menacing, overbearing teenager, who, encouraged by the expanding political influence of his father, was given to throwing his weight about not only amongst his companions but also amongst gullible railway employees. Ranga shuddered at the revelation that these were Jogu's friends. No wonder he was doing badly at school.

Ranga withdrew into the shadows and walked slowly to his quarter, wondering how to wean Jogu from the unwanted company of Vicky and his friends. Should he speak to Nagamma? No, he told himself. She will take it too seriously, and in her anxiety, may say or do something which could make matters worse. Deciding to keep the information to himself, he finished collecting the papers, without arousing Nagamma's suspicions. He returned home earlier than usual feigning a headache and lay down in the bedroom to await Jogu's return. The youngster came a little later and burst into the kitchen and loudly demanded his meal as he was ravenously hungry.

"Shh, Jogu, don't speak so loudly. Your father is down with a headache" Nagamma admonished him.

His mother's words had no effect on Jogu. They only irritated him further.

"You mean I have to remain hungry until his *vedhava* headache recedes?" he shouted, using the expletive he had been trained to avoid.

"Mind your language, Jogu" his mother said sharply, "I will serve you when I am ready. Now go to your room and wait."

Jogu emerged from the kitchen grumbling loudly cursing the house, his family and his fate, for keeping him hungry, his speech interspersed with Hindi expletives.

"Is that all or have you more kind words for us, My Lord?" interrupted Ranga.

A shocked expression crossed Jogu's face.

"Nanna garu!" he stuttered.

"Is this why we brought you into this world? Is this why we reared you lovingly, sent you to school and sacrificed our needs to make you happy? Is this house to be filled with the filthy abuse you have picked from your despicable friends? Answer me, you good for nothing slob."

Ranga spat out his reprimand in one breath. Jogu listened with his head bowed but at the mention of his friends he lifted his face and responded,

"Don't bring my friends into this, *nannagaru*" he said, petulantly.

It was enough to throw Ranga off balance. All the bottled-up resentment in Ranga exploded suddenly as he thundered,

"Your friends, did you say? That scoundrel Vikram, son of a corrupt contractor, and his *chamchas*, who have been teaching you to smoke pot? You call them your friends, and dare to stand up to your own father on their behalf?"

Ranga followed up this diatribe with a resounding slap which sent the boy sprawling on the floor, clutching his burning cheek. Nagamma ran out of the kitchen at the sound of Ranga's raised voice too late to stop the violence. She rushed to her son shouting at Ranga,

"Have you gone mad? You must have broken his jaw."

Jogu brushed aside his mother, picked himself up and ran to the safety of his room, covering his cheek with his palm.

Jogu sulked for the next few days while his cheek healed, refusing everything except the minimum of food. While Nagamma railed at Ranga for his rash action, Ranga cursed himself for losing control of himself. He had never hit Jogu, since he had entered his teens, fearing the emotional trauma it would cause him, but this time he had allowed his temper to get the better of him. He prayed to God to forgive him and help Jogu to get over it. But Jogu became incommunicative in the following months, speaking only to his mother to meet his essential needs, spending much of his time outside the house, revealing nothing of his activities. Ranga kept track of his movements and was relieved to find that he had parted ways with the company of his old chums, and instead was now very friendly with his classmate Avinash, who was the son of the local Assistant Engineer. Jogu seemed to have become more regular in his timings, and more interested in his studies. The boys spent long hours in Avinash's study, sometimes stretching beyond midnight. On these occasions Jogu would stay back overnight and return home only the next morning. Avinash's father, Satish Gupta and his wife assured Ranga that Jogu was safe and diligent. There is nothing to worry, Ranga told himself repeatedly, but an inexplicable fear refused to leave him.

The arrival of Avinash's cousin Tanmay introduced a new element in the activities of the boys. He was a student of IIT Kharagpur. The workers in the hostel's messes had gone on a lightning strike leaving the students to manage for themselves. The Institute was closed pending a settlement and the students advised to go home temporarily. On such occasions, which were not infrequent in Kharagpur, Tanmay came to his uncle's place in Chandichowki instead travelling to distant Ambala where his father was employed. He brought with him information about a new movement sweeping the state. Who were its leaders, what was their ideology, their objectives and their strategies? It was obvious to Avinash and his friends that Tanmay was not merely well informed. He was deeply involved. For students of IIT Kharagpur, and other colleges and universities, most of whom would be wearing out their footwear in search of jobs after graduation, the movement proved to be extremely attractive.

'But we don't know anything about weapons' the boys said.

'No problem. There is a place where training is given. Do you want to join?' Tanmay queried.

'Yes, yes we would like to' they replied.

Tanmay gave them the details of the training ground and a few days later returned to Kharagpur.

The boys kept their confabulations with Tanmay to themselves, giving their parents the impression that they were taking Tanmay's help in their studies.

When the government cracked down with the help of the army, teenagers were their first target. They were rounded up from homes, schools, colleges and hostels. In Chandichowki, they came looking for Jogu, Avinash and their friends. Avinash was arrested and taken away. Most of the youngsters whisked away by the police never returned. In a few cases, police informed the parents of the demise of their children, but many parents were left clueless. Ranga and Nagamma despaired of seeing Jogu but they refused to accept he was dead and never placed a garland on his portrait. On the advice of their gurus, they accepted their fate as the consequence of their actions in previous births, and showering all their love on their remaining child, focussed their lives on Radha's education and welfare. When Radha came of age, they began to look for a suitable groom for her.

◆———◆———◆

The prospective bridegroom, Shyamal Rao, was a software engineer based in USA. He was in India on a short visit and his parents had arranged for him to meet several prospective brides in the hope that he would find his life partner. He came with his parents Madhava Rao and Satyavati, older brother Ramakant and his wife Sushila. Ranga and Nagamma prepared for their visit carefully. Radha was dressed up at her best for the occasion. The meeting proceeded cordially and both sides agreed that the boy and girl were well matched. When asked about their opinions, Shyamal Rao nodded and Radha responded with a deep blush and a coy smile, throwing a sidelong glance at the 'boy'. While the celebratory sweets were being served,

Sushila pointed to the picture of a young boy on one of the walls that she had been contemplating, and asked,

"Who is in that picture, aunty?"

The colour drained from Nagamma's face and her lips quivered. Ranga came to her rescue,

"That's our son Joga Rao, Amma. He has been missing for some time."

Sushila exchanged glances with her husband and with Shyamal Rao. They got into a huddle and began to whisper among themselves and with Shyamal Rao's parents, as Ranga and Nagamma looked on with mounting impatience and apprehension. Ranga picked up courage to ask,

"What is the matter, Sir? Have we done something wrong?"

Madhava Rao suddenly realized that they had unnecessarily scared the hosts with their behavior.

"No, Ranga Rao garu" he tried to pacify Ranga, "please don't take it amiss. We were just wondering that your son bears a remarkable resemblance to someone we saw recently."

Ranga jumped up from his seat and Nagamma's wan face brightened up like a newly lit lamp.

"Where? Where did you see him?" Ranga asked, excitedly.

"Before coming here" said Madhava Rao, "we had gone to seek the blessings of our gurumata, Sadhvi Sharada Mataji in Deoghar. There, we met a disciple of Mataji and her son who looks just like your son."

For Ranga and Nagamma it was like rebirth. Radha could not hold her tears. Nagamma prayed to all the deities she could recall, to make it so that that boy turns out to be her long-lost son.

"Let us go there and bring him back home" she urged her husband.

"We do not know if he is our Jogu, but we must go and see him" he told her, and addressing Madhava Rao,

"Sir, this is very important for us. We would like to perform this wedding only after we meet this boy who looks like our son. Please help us to go there and see him."

"Shyamal has to return to USA in a week" said Ramakant.

"I can understand your emotions, Ranga Rao garu. I have a suggestion. Since my son and your daughter have agreed, why not perform the wedding ceremony in Mataji's Ashram? If that boy is indeed your son, Radha will get her brother's blessings as well."

Everyone agreed with this plan and they all travelled to Mataji's Ashram in Deoghar.

They reached Deoghar the next morning. The morning prayers were about to start when they arrived at the Ashram. Silently, they took the seats they were ushered to, but Ranga's family continued to be tormented by hope and uncertainty. They waited impatiently for the prayers to end so that they could resume their quest for Jogu. When they joined the singing of *Jaya Jagadeesh Hare* during *Aarti*, their spirits revived slightly, but the pain became a knot in the pit of their stomachs.

At the end of the *Aarti*, Madhava Rao led them out into the open and spoke to one of the *sevaks* to ask about Punmasi, the lady with whom they had seen Jogu's look-alike. When they found her and Madhava Rao asked her about her son, Punmasi called out,

"Birju *bitua*, see who has come to meet us."

"Did you call me, *maayi?*"

A young man came towards them, separating himself from the crowd. He had a slight limp and there were scars on his forehead, jaw and hands. His eyes lit up when he saw Madhava Rao and Satyavati. He moved to them quickly and bowed down to touch their feet. He glanced briefly at Ranga and Nagamma but showed no sign of recognition. Madhava Rao blessed him and as he stood up, Nagamma addressed him in Telugu,

"Jogu, my son, don't you remember your mother?"

The young man turned to Punmasi.

"Who are these people, *maayi?* What is she saying?"

Punmasi looked up to Madhava Rao for an answer. Madhava Rao explained to her that Ranga and Nagamma's son was missing and that they thought Birju might be that missing son.

Tears welled up from Punmasi's eyes.

"Is he really your son, Punmasiji?"

Punmasi wanted to say yes, but her sense of justice and fair play got the better of her, she replied slowly, trying to control herself.

"Yes, he is my son. But I did not bear him in my womb, although I wish I had."

"Then, how did he become your son?"

"Some years ago, we lived in Basdeopur in West Bengal, where my husband was working. We had no children. One day, on his way home from work, he found this boy lying in a roadside drain in a pool of blood. He had a gash on his head and injuries on his arms and legs. With the help of others, my husband took him to hospital. He told me that the boy had lost his memory and didn't know who he was and where he came from. We brought him home, gave him a name and cared for him like our own child. We moved to this Ashram after my husband retired. My husband died last year."

After a pause, she added,

"Maybe he is their child, but how can I live without him? He is my only support."

Ranga and Nagamma were now sure that Birju was indeed none other than Jogu. But Jogu did not know them and when Nagamma tried to ruffle his hair, he recoiled and tried to hide behind Punmasi. Nagamma broke down and sobbed hysterically. Radha went to Jogu and held his scar marked face in her hands,

"Bhayya, don't you remember your *chhoti bahen*? Show me your wrist. See, it still has the mark of my Rakhee."

Jogu's eyes moistened suddenly, but he shook his head and resumed his place behind Punmasi. Madhava Rao and his family watched the emotional scene silently. Madhava Rao patted Ranga's shoulder.

"Let us go and have *darshan* of Mataji first. It will make you feel better."

They joined the line of people waiting for *darshan* and waited. After some time one of the *sevaks* near Mataji announced on the public address system,

"Rangarao and Nagamma, please come for Mataji's *darshan.*"

Ranga was surprised to hear his name being announced. He wondered how they knew his name until he recalled that they had registered their names when they entered the Ashram. They were escorted by *sevaks* to where Mataji was seated in Padmasana, her eyes half closed. They placed offerings of flowers and fruits in containers placed near her and bowed low to Mataji with their hands folded. Mataji opened her eyes and looked at them. The serenity in her gaze calmed their aching hearts. She smiled and spoke in a deep voice that would stay with them forever.

"Don't take the child from the mother.

Don't keep the mother from the child."

They couldn't comprehend the import of the words but when they told Madhava Rao he knew the meaning at once.

"Don't you see?" he said, "Mataji wants you to stay in the Ashram. In that case Birju is not taken from his mother and Nagamma is not kept away from Jogu."

Ranga and Nagamma agreed immediately. The next few days were spent in arranging for the wedding of Radha with Shyamal Rao and in finding rooms for Ranga and Nagamma to stay in the Ashram. Punmasi and Birju joined them in the wedding ceremonies. At the time of parting, Radha took leave from her parents and touched Birju's feet. He hugged her fondly and she cried on his shoulder, shedding tears of grief for parting and of joy at finding her brother.

When Radha and Shyamal Rao returned to India two years later, they found the two families living together. Birju seemed to love Tauji and Badimayi, as he called Ranga and Nagamma, as much as his own Mayi and allowed them to call him Jogu. But Jogu never recalled his life in Chandichowki nor did he discover what had caused his injuries.

Perhaps, it was all for the best.

Doctor in the Soup

Dr. Joyendra Nath Mitra, Joy to his friends, the Divisional Medical Officer of Dharampur Division, was on the horns of a dilemma.

The Divisional Superintendent had issued written orders that no officer of his Division would travel to Calcutta under any circumstances without his personal approval. Officers had to go to Calcutta often for umpteen jobs in the zonal headquarters, as well as in other offices. Sometimes, they had to attend meetings and conferences arranged by departmental chiefs and others. The travelling allowance rates being much higher in the metropolis, officers and others often made the trip for minor tasks, causing unwarranted outflow of funds. To curb this tendency, all divisions had imposed restrictions on travelling to Calcutta, under instructions from the zonal office. But sometimes, officers sought to justify such journeys on the strength of a message, manoeuvred from an official in headquarters.

In Dharampur Division, the DS's way of implementing the orders was much more abrasive. He made it mandatory for everyone to obtain his prior permission for attending any meeting in the zonal headquarters. This caused considerable resentment, because it meant that the officers had to seek his approval even for the periodical review meetings called by the heads of their departments, although the DS held a lower rank than the HODs and could not, therefore, interfere with their orders.

Unfortunately for Joy, the Chief Medical Officer had fixed a conference of medical officers on the same day that the DS had himself called a meeting of the Branch Officers (BOs) of Dharampur Division. He could neither skip the CMO's conference nor excuse himself from the DS's meeting. Eventually, he decided to prefer his own departmental head, who was himself a tyrant, and sent a note to the DS, seeking his permission to travel to Calcutta to attend the conference, scheduled for the Monday following the forthcoming weekend. To make it palatable, Joy not only apologised for his absence at the branch officers' meeting, but also mentioned he would take advantage of his visit to further one of the DS's pet schemes on family welfare.

After sending the note, Joy felt confident that the DS would fall for his gambit and so lost no time in arranging for his visit. He was, therefore, more than surprised when the file was returned to him late on

Thursday, with the word *Regret* scrawled in red ink across the space at the bottom of his note. With just three days left for the conference, Joy was in a quandary. He dared not displease the CMO, but he couldn't go to Calcutta without the consent of DS. There was no question of absenting himself from the Divisional meeting. There was no knowing what the DS would do to get even. He called Dr. Prashanto Sen, the Dy CMO, whose broad shoulders were used by all field medical officers to sob out their woes. Dr. Sen told him that CMO had arranged the conference in preparation for a bigger conference of CMOs in New Delhi, which would be addressed by the Railway Minister. The CMO would, therefore, be very upset if he did not attend the zonal conference. He strongly advised Joy to explain the importance of the conference to the DS and persuade him to allow Joy to attend it. But that was easier said than done.

When Khushwant Singh Talwar became DS of Dharampur Division he found himself in a hostile environment in an alien railway infested with rivals, who surrounded him like sharks, waiting to tear him to pieces if he made the slightest error of judgment. Eager to establish himself, he drove his bunch of very talented, hand-picked officers like a slave driver, giving no quarter, accepting no excuse. If he was aware of their intrinsic qualities and commitment to performance, he kept it strictly to himself.

His day would begin with a call from Gautam Chakravarty, the Chief Controller, who headed the organization that monitored the movement of trains over the division. His task was to brief the DS of the performance of the previous day, explaining shortfalls and pointing out the defaulters responsible for them. It was a daunting task. Talwar would interrupt him repeatedly, questioning facts, doubting explanations, and suspecting Chakravarty's loyalty. At the end of the conversation, Gautam babu would emerge battered and bruised in spirit. He would gulp his coffee, which would become lukewarm while he talked to Talwar, collect himself, and set out to face the day.

Armed with the facts and figures garnered from Gautam babu, Talwar would commence his assault on his branch officers. He would tackle each of them not only using the information he already had from the chief controller, but also what he gathered from the BOs, playing them against each other. Lastly, he would call Sridhar, the Divisional Operating Superintendent (DOS), confront him with what he thought were the failures of the previous day and seek an explanation. In Talwar's view, Sridhar was a follower of his arch rival Sailab Singh, popularly known as 'Genius', who was DS of the adjacent Division. He, therefore, distrusted Sridhar and tried every means to discover shortcomings in his work. Despite all his manipulative skills, Talwar could never pin Sridhar down on any subject. Quietly efficient and well informed, Sridhar would listen to Talwar and counter his accusations, cutting through his arguments like a skilled surgeon. Talwar was irritated by Sridhar's unruffled attitude. Today, he thought he had the ammunition to blast that calm.

He called up Sridhar and began aggressively.

"I say, what is going on? Why are we sending out light engines?"

When locomotives ran without hauling loads, they were called light engines.

"We didn't need them at the time, Sir," replied Sridhar, coolly. "Besides, we were under orders from the Dy Goods."

The Deputy Chief of Operations in charge of goods train operations was usually referred to by his short name of Dy Goods. Talwar didn't like him. He was another of those sharks, out for Talwar's blood. He was sure the orders were issued just to make things difficult for Talwar, and the Division he headed.

"Does your friend think we can run trains without powers?" Talwar continued his attack. He meant motive powers.

"We are not short of powers, Sir. Moreover, holding more locos will only depress our loco utilisation index."

Talwar saw the logic of the argument but was not about to give up. He raised his voice and spoke rudely.

"So, you think you can get away with looking after others, ignoring this Division's needs?"

This was too much for Sridhar. There was steel in his voice as he replied in kind.

"Why don't you speak to 'my friend', as you call him, for a change? And if you think I am not working for you, you may like to ask the Chief to replace me."

Sridhar dropped the telephone without waiting for Talwar's permission.

Aware of the reputation Sridhar had built up for himself on the railway, Talwar was left with no choice but to seethe within himself. He arrived in his office in a foul temper, his bushy eyebrows knitted together in a frown, his peach coloured cheeks assuming the hue of ripe tomatoes, his pink lips curled up and ready to hurl the most vitriolic abuse at any one who dared to cross his path.

Unaware of Talwar's brush with Sridhar, Joy, assuming the DS would be more relaxed and, therefore, more receptive and kindly disposed in the morning, turned up a few minutes later. He was in for a rude shock.

Talwar's peon, Rahman, had gone to the Office Superintendent to report his arrival. Joy noticed the red indicator light above the DS's door, but, based on his experience in other divisions, did not treat it as a bar to the entry of branch officers like himself. He pushed the door ajar and inserted his head into the opening.

Talwar was sitting with his head bent over some papers on his table.

"Good morning, Sir. May I come in?" said Joy.

Talwar raised his head. His bloodshot eyes looked through the intruder, as if he was some transparent substance. His face became red like a piece of ham. Instead of answering Joy's simple question, he placed his finger on the calling bell button and kept pressing it. The shrill, ceaseless peals of the DS's electrical calling bell filled the corridors of the office building and spilled into the adjoining rooms. It reached Sripat Mishra, the Office Superintendent, and the peon, Rahman. While the latter returned to his post on the double, the former followed him at a speed unusual for one so bulky.

Rahman noticed the doctor. Gently pushing him aside, he entered the DS's chamber. He was greeted by a tirade uttered in a loud, quivering voice.

"Where did you disappear?" Talwar demanded. "How dare you leave your place of duty without my permission?"

Rahman explained in a respectful tone that he had gone to report the DS's arrival to the Office Superintendent. Talwar flared up.

"What is the use of reporting my arrival when the whole world has already come to know?" he shouted adding a few choice expletives, in the course of which, Rahman was severally anointed with epithets like idiot, inept, imbecile, faithless, disloyal, and accused of lacking in respect, neglecting his duties etc.

While this diatribe was in progress, Sripat Babu reached the DS's room. Joy, who was still standing at the door, had to push it open further to allow the wider frame of the OS to enter, and in the process found himself sandwiched between the peon and the Babu. After he had exhausted the list of names he could recall, Talwar resumed his nagging attitude, continuing to address his peon.

"So, you think I have nothing better to do here in the morning, except meeting people with their petty requests?"

They listened to him in silence, standing opposite him, with their backs to the wall. After a long pause Talwar began again. This time the target was Sripat

Mishra. Talwar accused him of being unmindful of his boss's needs, allowing all and sundry to disturb him at their will.

"People suffer from diseases, while I suffer from my OS", he groaned.

The session was interrupted when the telephone rang and the operator told Talwar about an important incoming call. Talwar gave a dismissive stare at the trio before him and took the call. As they trooped out, Rahman and Sripat exchanged meaningful glances. They did not seem to be any the worse after the treatment they had just received from their boss. It dawned on Joy that, although Talwar had not spoken to him directly, all the abuses and complaints were directed towards him. And the peon and the OS knew it!

After this incident Joy made several more attempts to meet Talwar but Talwar was either out on tour or too preoccupied to meet his DMO. Joy began to become desperate. On Saturday, Talwar was in town but he was tied up with the visit of a high official from the Railway Board, who would be lunching with Talwar in the latter's sprawling bungalow. With apprehension in his heart and the file in his hand, Joy reached the DS's bungalow. The peon, who stopped him at the door saying the boss was busy, melted at the kind doctor's entreaties and seeing the agony in his eyes. He went over to where Talwar was sitting, chatting with his guest, and whispered something in his ears. Talwar rose, visibly annoyed at this interruption and came to the door.

"Yes?" he said testily.

Joy blabbered out his rehearsed speech, explaining the reason for his unwelcome visit. Talwar cut him short curtly.

"So, you think that justifies your disturbing me when I am entertaining an important guest?"

He snatched the file from Joy, placed it on top of a nearby bookcase, out of the doctor's reach, and turned his back on him dismissively. Joy remained standing at the door, shocked at Talwar's lack of civility. When, after what seemed an eternity to him, Joy eventually turned to go, he was surprised to hear a familiar voice.

"Hello, Doc. Fancy meeting you here?"

Joy looked back over his shoulder and found the 'important guest' standing behind him and smiling at him kindly, with his hand extended in greeting. He was none other than Pramod Shukla, erstwhile Divisional Superintendent of a Division on the Northern zone, where Joy was posted earlier. A pleasant, amiable person by nature, Shukla had a special reason to remember Dr. Mitra. For the first time in several days,

Joy felt a taste of real happiness. He grasped Shukla's hand and pressed it in gratitude.

"How are you, Sir? I am now DMO Dharampur."

Shukla turned to Talwar, who stood behind Shukla, looking lost at this display of familiarity between his guest and his subordinate.

"Did you know that Dr. Mitra is an exceedingly good surgeon? When my son was suddenly attacked with diphtheria, he performed the emergency operation to save his life."

Joy noticed a sudden change in Talwar. It was amazing. Talwar seemed to have shed his earlier personality like a snake shedding its skin. The scowl, the blazing eyes and the up-curled lip that had confronted Joy only a few minutes ago, disappeared miraculously from Talwar's face. They were replaced by a smile that spread up to Talwar's ears, with the eyes joining in the fun.

"Why didn't you tell me you knew Mr. Shukla so well? I would have invited you to join in the lunch."

Joy looked on tongue-tied, unable to believe his eyes.

"It is not too late even now. Join us for lunch."

Joy found his tongue at last.

"Thank you very much, Sir" he managed to mumble, "but I cannot stay. My family is waiting for me."

"Then you must join us for the soup" Talwar insisted, looking at Shukla, as though he wanted his approval. The latter nodded and looked encouragingly at Joy. Unwilling to displease either of them, he acceded, albeit reluctantly, and took a seat. After making the usual personal enquiries, Pramod Shukla turned back to Talwar to resume the conversation, interrupted by Mitra's unwanted arrival. Ignored by the seniors, Joy remained sitting. The cushions under him felt like stones, and the arms of the chair like hot irons. He wanted to get up and go away, but how could he leave without solving the problem that had brought him here in the first place? But the two persons beside him seemed oblivious of his urgency. The file he had brought with him remained where Talwar had placed it. Joy looked at it longingly. He did not dare to rise and pick up the file.

Talwar's bearer came in with a tray carrying soup for the guests. Shukla and Talwar picked up their cups without a pause in their discussion. The bearer thrust the tray under Joy's face. He took his cup and silently took a sip.

It tasted like ash.

Mind Your Language

In early spring sometime in the late 1950s, thirty-seven callow youth converged on the city of Baroda, later renamed Vadodara, to launch their careers. They were the newly recruited officers known by the high sounding and unduly long, but to them meaningless, designation of, "Officers of the Superior Revenue Establishment of the Traffic (Transportation) and Commercial Departments of Indian Railways", shortened to TT & CD. During their training period, they were known as Probationary Officers or simply probationers. On receipt of their appointment orders, they had reported to General Managers of the zonal railways to which they were allotted. They had now been deputed to attend their first training course together in the Railway Staff College in Baroda.

They came from across the country and spoke different languages, and they spoke English with accents peculiar to their regions. Those who had gone to mission schools and colleges spoke in the clipped tones the British masters had handed down to them. They were from different social classes, scions of bureaucrats, lawyers, teachers, businessmen, government servants and railway employees. Despite these differences, they were one in their desire to make their contribution to building the new India of their dreams.

Freed from the British yoke just a decade ago, when these officers were students, they had keenly watched the country take infant steps to overcome the abysmal state of the economy, exploited by colonists for two centuries, its infrastructure devastated by overuse and neglect of maintenance during the second World War. Fired by the zeal instilled in them by the leaders of the independence movement, who now held the reins of power, they were eagerly awaiting their assigned responsibilities in building the nation.

Democracy was taking roots slowly. In the first two general elections, voter turnouts had been less than 50 % and, as some of the officers in this group learnt from firsthand experience while working in the polling booths in the last election, voters in rural areas were confused about their roles and feared approaching the ballot box. Many of the first lot of leaders were idealists with visions of greatness for the country, selfless patriots who had sacrificed their careers and their wealth for the freedom struggle.

The party had developed the agenda for progress after independence but there was no unanimity as to means and ends. An important item in the agenda of the party was the formation of linguistic states. Soon after the formation of the new government a senior bureaucrat, in a bid to prove his nationalist credentials, reminded the new Home Minister of a report submitted by a committee of senior freedom fighters, some of whom were now in the cabinet, recommending the formation of linguistic states immediately after independence. The astute Home Minister told him to keep the report on the shelf. He didn't want to disturb a hornet's nest when the country had more important challenges to face.

A few years down the line, however, matters came to a head when a respected freedom fighter, sitting on hunger strike in support of a separate state for Telugu speaking people, was ignored by the government and forfeited his life. The agitations that followed forced the government to concede the formation of the Andhra state and to appoint a committee to reorganize states on linguistic lines. Based on the report of the committee, state boundaries were redrawn, new capitals were created and some of the old capitals relegated to the status of provincial towns. Nevertheless, linguistic and regional chauvinism was yet to gain the notoriety it gained in subsequent years. Hindi movies and their songs continued to be popular in South India, south

Indians tried to learn the meaning of the lilting numbers from Hindi films, and north Indian film stars were as sought after as homebred heroes.

The new arrivals were received and registered in a booth set up at the railway station and escorted to the Railway Staff College by designated staff and ushered to their hostels. Classes commenced the next day with an introductory welcome speech, followed by their first lecture. At the tea break, the trainees mingled and got to know each other, standing together in small groups sipping tea. Kamal Jharia from Ranchi was in a group with three others when he noticed a probationer talking fluently in English and Urdu, interspersed with Urdu couplets. He had a North Indian accent like someone from UP. Seeing his lanky, dark frame Kamal concluded that he was a Muslim from Aligarh. He tried to recall the names of the probationers in the class but could not recollect a Muslim name. Maybe his name was in another letter of appointment which he was not aware of. He decided to wait for the next day and see to which name he responds during roll call. The next day Kamal strained his eyes and ears to hear the probationer respond to a Muslim name but could not catch his quarry answering the call. On the third day, Kamal kept his eyes glued on the probationer as the roll was called. He was shocked to hear him say, "Present, Sir" to the call of Manohar Rao. Kamal waited restlessly for the tea break and making straight for the probationer, confronted him with the words,

"Your name cannot be Manohar Rao!"

It was Manohar Rao's turn to be shocked.

"Why? What do you find objectionable in my name?" he said, without hiding his irritation.

"Sorry, I didn't mean it that way" said Kamal extending his hand and smiling, "I am Kamal Jharia from Ranchi. You are so fluent in Urdu, I assumed you are from Aligarh."

Manohar Rao took the extended hand and shook it warmly before responding.

"Thank you for the compliment. I happen to have grown up in a Hindi speaking area. I went to Hindi Primary and Middle Schools. So, I am more proficient in Hindi than in my mother tongue."

"And Urdu?"

"Entirely self-taught. I fell in love with the poetry on hearing it from a friend and followed it up by reading."

"Fascinating. Like to know more about it, if you don't mind."

"You are welcome" said Manohar Rao.

One of the teachers pulled the children out of their class rooms and rushed them home. When they reached the *Brahmana Veethi*, the short narrow street where the Brahmins of the village lived, the children saw a crowd in front of their house and heard loud wailing. The teacher escorted them carefully, skirting the crowd to enter the house. Twelve-year old Hari sensed the cause of the commotion and taking Manohar, his younger ten-year old sibling firmly by the hand, sidled to a corner of the room and settled on the floor. Tears spurted from his eyes involuntarily as he addressed Manohar,

"*Peddananna* is dead I think."

Hari and Mohan were in Padmavaram, the village where their maternal aunt Ganga lived with her family. Their uncle Sitaramayya, whom they called *Peddananna* was a teacher in the local school. Their parents Shankar Rao and Lakshmi, Ganga's younger sister, lived in the Central Provinces where Shankar was employed at Kanhapur, a small railway station. There were no schools near the station and the nearest one in the neighbouring cantonment town of Amargarh, taught in the Hindi medium. Shankar and Lakshmi wanted their children to learn Telugu. When approached, Ganga and Sitaramayya readily agreed to host the boys.

The children soon discovered that *Peddananna* was bitten by a snake when he was trying to clean the backyard. All attempts to prevent the poison from spreading had failed. It was no longer possible for Ganga to bear the burden of two additional children apart from her own brood of five. Reluctantly, on the advice of the village elders, she arranged to escort the children back to their parents. And that was the end of their Telugu education.

Back in Kanhapur, Shankar took them to the Hindi medium school in Amargarh. Initially, the Head Master insisted on taking them only in the lowest class, but when Shankar promised to get them privately coached in Hindi, he agreed to admit them in higher classes. Hari did well and Manu, as Manohar was called, excelled in all subjects, including Hindi, in the first half-yearly examination and earned a promotion to the next grade. The parents heaved a sigh of relief and decided to abandon the idea of educating their children in Telugu.

In due course, the children outgrew the schools in Amargarh and moved to the city of Narayanpur for further education. English was the medium of instruction, local languages being relegated to second language. Preferring to study physical sciences, the children dropped Hindi in the middle school. But the interest ignited in the language remained and they read Bhartendu Harischandra, Jaya Shankar Prasad, Prem Chand and modern poets, Sumitranandan Pant, Nirala and Bachchan with as much zeal and learning as Shakespeare, Scott, Wordsworth, Byron, Shelley and Keats. Fluency in speaking Hindi was a natural by product.

Manu's friends complimented him on his diction, and he was often mistaken for a North Indian. During a study tour in Andhra Pradesh with a group of North Indian students, he lapsed into his mother tongue to give directions to the driver. When he resumed his seat, one of the students complimented him,

"Manuji, you speak the local language fluently."

They were amazed to learn that it was his mother tongue.

After his post-graduation, Manu was offered a temporary teaching assignment in a college in Madhya Pradesh. Soon afterwards, he had to attend an interview for selection for the job. The Principal of the Science College, Narayanpur, where Manu had studied, was a member of the interview panel. The Madhya Pradesh government had declared Hindi as the official language and made it compulsory for all employees to know it. It was, therefore, expected that candidates would be questioned about their knowledge of the language. South Indians prepared to answer the question,

"*kyaa aap Hindi jaante hain?*" (Do you know Hindi?),

with a pre rehearsed reply,

"haan main Hindi bolnaa aur padhnaa jaanta hoon." (Yes, I can speak and read Hindi.)

During the interview, the Principal, himself a South Indian with sparse knowledge of Hindi, finished asking technical questions before asking Manu to explain the first law of thermodynamics in Hindi. The Chairman of the panel intervened with the question,

"Rao Sahib, *aap Hindi padh likh sakte hain?"* (Mr Rao, do you know Hindi?)

"jee haan" (Yes, Sir)

replied Manu, without hesitation, using the conversational style of reply in Hindi.

The Chairman smiled,

"He says *jee haan,* Principal Sahib, there is no need to test him further."

———◆———

"That's amazing, Manohar Rao" said Kamal.

"Not quite" replied Manohar, "I am sure there are many like me. Their stories might differ in detail. It doesn't always go one way, though. Sometimes, it can be just the reverse."

"What do you mean?"

"Wait till you hear this story."

———◆———

When the Madhya Pradesh government declared Hindi as the official language, it also mandated that all government servants should clear an examination to test their knowledge of the language. Those who failed to do so would be denied their next increment and confirmation in the job they were holding. The Government also decided to introduce Hindi medium in the teaching of science subjects. A Committee headed by Dr. Raghuveer had compiled a dictionary of scientific terms in Hindi for this purpose. For teaching staff, the Hindi test included questions on the new vernacular terminology. Only those whose mother tongue was Hindi and others who had taken Hindi as a subject in the Matriculation Examination or had obtained the Sahitya Visharad degree from the Rashtra Bhasha Prachar Samiti, were exempted.

Manohar Rao was not perturbed. Initially, he toyed with the idea of appearing for the Visharad examination, but he dismissed it because he was already preparing for the Civil Services examinations and this would eat into his study time. There was not much in the Hindi test anyway, a few translations and compositions which he could handle with ease.

The other candidates for the test included Phadnis and Paranjpe from Maharastra, Ganesan from Tamil Nadu and Syed Abidi, Professor of Persian and Arabic. Knowing Manu's facility with the language, all of them asked for his help and he gave them tips to clear the test. Prof Abidi's knowledge of Hindi was so poor that he found it difficult to answer the questions, despite Manu's advice. During the test, the organisers left the examinees without an invigilator, esteeming their position as teachers. Struggling with his compositions as time was running out, Prof Abidi begged for help but Manu ignored him as he was busy completing his answers, but when he had done, Prof Abidi pulled out Manu's answer sheet and copied the contents into his sheet as Manu watched helplessly.

The result of the test was announced after a month. Ganesan broke the news to Manu, with downcast glances.

"All of us cleared the test, Manohar, except you."

"What?" exclaimed Manu in disbelief.

Ganesan nodded silently.

"And Abidi?" asked Manu.

"He has passed too" replied Ganesan.

It took Manu some time to recover from the unexpected setback. He prepared for the next test with diligence and caution avoiding contact with other examinees. A new item was added to the test. Candidates were asked to read a handwritten manuscript in Hindi. When it was Manu's turn, he took the manuscript, read it in one breath and returned it to the examiner. Impressed by the performance, the examiner remarked in Hindi,

"Rao Sahib, aapki Hindi bahut achhi hai. Phir aap pichhli baar paas kyun nahi huwe?" (Mr Rao, your Hindi is very good. How come you didn't pass the last time?)

"ye tho aap hi bataa sakte hain, panditji" replied Manu. (Only you can answer that question, Sir)

As Manu left the room, the second examiner in the panel of examiners revealed that when he was correcting the answer sheets of the last test, he had noticed that the compositions submitted by two of the candidates were identical. One was written by a Muslim professor and the other by a South Indian. It seemed obvious that the South Indian had copied the composition written by the Muslim. Accordingly, the Muslim was passed and the South Indian failed.

Made in the USA
Monee, IL
30 January 2020

21068266R00083